Junction 2020
Book One: The Portal

Carol Riggs

Carolyn—
thanks so much
for your critiquing
& reading!
Best,
Carol
Riggs

Junction 2020 Book One: The Portal
Copyright 2010
by Carol Ann Riggs

Cover Artwork designed by Carol Riggs, with special
thanks to Gabby Cornelia for having her arm
photographed.

ISBN: 1453730877
EAN-13: 9781453730874

For Dennis, who gives me support and makes it
possible for me to write,
and for my daughters Janelle and Megan.
For my niece Emily, who always read my early novels--
including the first version of this one.

Acknowledgments

I would like to express my thanks to these writer friends who have taken the time to review and critique this novel: Barbara Herkert, Carolyn Short, and Patricia Bailey. Also to my mom, Betty Hazel, for her extra-sharp proofreading skills.

Junction 2020

Chapter 1

New Year's Eve, 2019. Nine o'clock at last. Mari Stratton snapped a checkered cloth over a table, exhaling with impatience as it billowed like a sail over uncharted waters for a suspended moment before settling into place. She threw on a white flash of napkins, added a hasty clanking of silverware, and returned the Parmesan and hot pepper shakers to their rightful places next to the wall.

There. Her shift, completed. Another efficient and industrious evening at Aunt Lacey and Uncle Jim's pizza restaurant. Too bad her father wasn't around to take notice. She really could do more than read adventure and romance novels in the backyard hammock.

She hurried past Uncle Jim in the kitchen, through the thick smells of sizzling pepperoni, pungent jalapeños and steamy detergent. In the cramped employee bathroom, she changed into jeans and a powder-blue top. Her reflection in the mirror frowned like a grumpy evil twin as she checked her make-up. And now, time for that blasted party. She would've much rather spent New Year's Eve with only Lauren and one or two other friends. But Lauren was a junior and wanted to go to Stefanie Anders' big End of the Year Bash.

Honestly. The things a person did in order to keep new friends.

Mari ran fingers through her layered dark hair, threw on her jacket, and dashed out the back door to the car. Her mother stood there in a waitress outfit, handing the Chevy keys to Randall as though relinquishing control of the known world to a chimpanzee. Randall looked scrubbed and shaved, his brown hair spiked to flawless precision. Mari rolled her eyes. All for Stefanie's benefit, she'd bet. He'd been unsuccessfully trying to impress Stefanie since September.

Randall kicked the tire as Mari climbed into the front seat. "And why do I have to drive *her* there?" he asked their mother with a jerk of his thumb at Mari. "Arriving with my sister and her deaf friend is such a loser thing to do."

Their mother's eyes narrowed. "You could always go back inside and start washing dishes."

"Fine, I'm leaving," Randall growled. He hopped into the car and revved the engine to life. Cranking the wheel, he spun out of the alley with a spray of gravel, leaving the sight of their mother with her arms folded into an incredibly peeved pretzel.

"And for your information," Mari notified Randall as he turned onto the street, "Lauren is hearing impaired, not deaf."

He shrugged. "Same diff. Man, are you that hard up for friends?"

"I don't see you hanging out with a whole herd of new buddies."

A muscle on the side of Randall's face twitched. He grunted and said nothing more.

Mari selected a Jaisha song from the music download menu to cover the bristling silence. She tapped her foot to the steady rhythm, watching cold skeletons of maple and oak trees file by her window in a Halloween-like procession. After a few minutes Randall screeched to a halt at Lauren's duplex. As Mari reached for the door handle, he hammered out two jolting blasts on the horn. Mari flinched.

"Think she'll hear that?" Randall said with a smirk.

"You're such a brain-challenged speck of nothing," Mari said. She turned to see Lauren's tall, graceful figure darting down the sidewalk. Yes, apparently Lauren had heard.

"Hi, Mari," Lauren said, sliding into the back seat. She adjusted her hearing-aid buds in her ears, where they perched like tiny beige snails.

"Hi, this is my brother Randall," Mari said, twisting so Lauren could read her lips. Just in case the helpful snails didn't pick up all the sound waves. "He's a junior, too."

"Nice to meet you, Randall," Lauren chirped.

Randall gave a hesitant wave toward the back seat. "Yeah, right," he mumbled.

He was being a jerk, but Mari knew how he felt. Even after four months, she was confused herself. Lauren didn't have that flat, tone-deaf quality to her voice when she talked. Probably because she hadn't begun to lose sounds until she'd been six. It was hard to tell how much Lauren actually heard, or how much she picked up from lip reading and context.

They drove out of town. The silhouette of the Anders' house loomed against the night sky long before they reached it. Glowing white lights left over from Christmas bordered every roofline and gable, plunging the rest of the house into dim, unknown spaces. Neighboring fields surrounded the home's tidy lawn. The long fieldgrass rippled in the wind, alive and writhing with shadows.

Mari felt a tingling sense of apprehension grow with the proximity of the house. Yes, very ghoulish and unnerving. But more importantly, what if her ex, Brad, showed up at this party? She didn't want to see him, not after the way he'd dumped her for Susan DeBarge last month.

Randall parked on the street at the end of a long line of cars. They walked to the house, where a bearded man holding a shimmering drink answered the doorbell.

"Come in!" the man boomed over thumping music. "I'm Mr. Anders, father and chaperone. Help yourself to the party!" He ushered them in with an exaggerated wink and a few unsteady steps.

Randall shot toward a table loaded with food, while Mari and Lauren drifted around until they ended up in the largest room. A live DJ mixed tunes there, and a gadget near the ceiling showered a constant smattering of glitter upon the dancers. Lauren, determined to join in, adjusted her hair to hide her hearing aids. She tapped a thin, freckled guy on the shoulder and motioned to the dance floor. They drifted off together.

Mari stood against the wall with her eyes half-closed while the music thrummed through her. The extreme bass reverberated within her body, feeling as though it reached to her bone marrow. Usually she loved to dance, but not right now. It hadn't helped that she'd seen Brad and Susan splashing around like cozy dolphins in the indoor swimming pool. Guys. Worthless beasts. Smile and kiss you one minute, discard you like last week's leftovers the next. It reminded her of her father, now living in newfound bliss in Florida with his ample-chested stockbroker...while her mother had fled to Stratton's Pizzeria to volunteer for waitressing slavery.

Mari's interest in romance novels was starting to curdle. She knew how romances *really* ended.

With a sigh, she checked her watch. Only ten-thirty. On the dance floor Lauren sashayed with a junior named Tony Rodriguez, gazing at him with dreamy eyes. Huh-oh. Instant heartbreak alert. At school Tony seemed to be one of those chick-magnet kinds of guys, always laughing with a flock of girls. Carelessly combed black hair, brown-sugar skin, and dark

10

romantic eyes. The droolable but dangerous type. She'd have to warn Lauren.

And earlier Randall had scored a dance with Stefanie--his "perfect" honor roll blonde--but Mari didn't see him now. Stefanie, however, strolled toward her, tucking silky hair behind ears that featured more earrings than a jewelry display rack. Pierced to cartilage and beyond. Stefanie's entourage of preppy girls mimicked her hair motions and lethargic sway.

"Oh, my," Stefanie said, catching sight of Mari. "If it isn't the sophomore, come to play interpreter and moral support for Lauren Carnes." Amazing, how such a velvety voice could sound so cutting.

"Lauren's doing fine by herself, thank you," Mari said with a nod to the dance floor.

White-blonde hair splaying, Stefanie turned. "Ah. I see, Tony Rodriquez...." She sauntered away, keeping the pair in her sights.

Mari frowned. No telling what Stefanie would do. Mari eyed Lauren and Tony, who danced with soft smiles upon their faces. No telling what Tony would do, either. Mari hurried over to Lauren as the song ended, but Mr. Anders' voice boomed out from the speakers before she could say anything. His words sounded a little slurred. Apparently, he kept his own stash of special punch somewhere.

"Listen up, everyone! Outside we're starting a New Year's Eve hunt before the midnight countdown begins. Dozens of golden ping-pong balls are hidden in the yard and fields. The more you find, the better prizes you win. An extra prize for the one who collects the most. Anyone who's interested, meet me out on the back deck."

"Sounds fun," Tony said, a daredevil gleam flashing in his eyes. "It's pitch black out there. You sweet ladies gonna try that with me?"

Lauren smiled a euphoric smile. "Sure, Tony."

"Well, actually--" Mari began, surprised he'd included her in the invitation.

Stefanie's smooth voice broke in as she sauntered over in a bright red jacket. "There you are, Tony-kins. Would you escort me outside for the hunt? We'll leave Mari and her deaf friend to enjoy the dance floor and the munchies table."

Tony's face registered bewilderment and dismay. "What--Lauren's *deaf?*" He craned his neck to stare back at Lauren while Stefanie led him away by the arm.

A pink flush washed over Lauren's face, and she looked at her feet.

Mari touched Lauren's arm, catching her eye. "Come on, want to do the hunt with me?"

"Okay," Lauren said, pressing her mouth into a thin line.

They set off for the back deck. An hour later found them gripping flashlights, peering as the glows illuminated a half-rotted stump in the field behind the house. Beams of wavering lights appeared like random ghosts in the smudgy darkness, winking out without warning as hunters darted behind bushes and small hilly areas. Abrupt shrieks and peals of laughter echoed across the wind-rippled fieldgrass.

Mari shivered. Brrr. Too bad they'd left their jackets in the house. She was collecting more goosebumps than ping-pong balls.

"Here's one," Lauren cried, leaping for a golden gleam by the stump. She deposited a spray-painted ping-pong ball into a bag she held.

Mari pointed the flashlight at her own face so Lauren could see her speak. "Are you ready to go back yet?"

Lauren shook her head. "No. We need twenty-five to earn a DVD. Let's check by those big bushes over there."

"Twenty-five?" Mari exclaimed. "That's six more to find. Aren't you cold?"

Either not hearing her or ignoring her, Lauren strode off, heading farther from the house.

Mari blew out an exasperated breath. Long tentacles of grass whipped her jeans legs as she waded after Lauren. She strained to see. They'd lost most of the light from the house, and now only the pale beams of their flashlights lit their way. She arrived at the bushes and saw Lauren disappear around the other side. A small golden orb nestled in the grass near Mari's feet. Aha. Lauren had missed that one, going too fast. She reached under a branch for the ball, and felt something skitter across her hand. She jerked her hand back, giving a strangled scream.

"Are you okay?" Lauren's voice called from the other side.

"I guess." Mari aimed the flashlight at her hand. Nothing there. Just her hand, shaking a little. "I got freaked out," she called out, feeling foolish. "Probably a leaf, but I thought it was a spider."

Lauren laugh echoed. "Spiders are little and shy. They won't hurt you."

"Right." Mari shuddered. Disgusting, spiders. With their scrambling, multiple legs and wicked bloodthirsty habits. They bit people all the time, and even if they didn't bite, she didn't want the nasty things crawling on her. How many spiders lurked in this field, anyway, thousands? Millions? Her teeth chattering, she snatched up the ping-pong ball and thrashed to join Lauren. When she circled the bushes, Lauren wasn't there.

13

"Lauren?"

No answer.

"Lauren--where are you?" she called, louder. A different kind of panic leaped inside her. She couldn't even see Lauren's flashlight beam. Had Lauren stumbled and fallen? Darkness crowded around Mari's pathetic swath of battery-operated light, pressing upon her skin like something solid.

"Lauren!" she yelled.

Sudden light bobbed fifteen feet away. "I'm right here, don't shout," Lauren said.

Mari squinted. Lauren had been behind a corner of something, a small structure. She hiked over to see Lauren investigating the exterior of a tool or supply shed. Surely the Anders family hadn't bothered to hide ping-pong balls in this remote little shed. She certainly wasn't going to check. Lots of gloomy places for spiders to lurk in there.

Unfortunately, Lauren had other ideas.

"Lauren, wait--" Mari said, as Lauren creaked open the door and disappeared inside. Mari groaned. For Pete's sake, what was wrong with that girl? Did she have no common sense, no instinct for self-preservation? Lauren's feet clunked across the shed floorboards. Off to the right in the field, a pair of light beams advanced toward them. Other treasure hunters. "We might have company pretty soon," Mari called.

Lauren didn't answer.

Mari rolled her eyes toward the inky blankness of the sky. She supposed she'd better help check out this shed, to speed things up. As she eased inside, the distant tweeting of a whistle sounded, announcing five minutes before the hunt ended. They'd have to get back soon.

The shed smelled musty, damp. Mari's nose tickled.

14

Dust-covered shelves on both sides were stacked with indiscernible things. Lauren shuffled near one shelf, off to the right. "Hey," Mari said. "The whistle blew. That means it's eleven-forty."

Lauren held up a golden ball in triumph. "Found one."

"Cool. Twenty-one, now." Mari added the ball in her own hand to Lauren's bag. Had Lauren heard what she'd said about the whistle? They couldn't miss the midnight countdown. After all, it wasn't every year the date changed to something as major and earth-shaking as 2020.

Although on second thought if Brad and Susan joined the crowd to celebrate the new year with an enthusiastic kiss, maybe she didn't care so much.

They found two more balls on the shelves, then Lauren ran her flashlight beam over the back of the shed to reveal a stool and a workbench. Odd geometric sketches and chunks of wood lay on the workbench, as well as a box of nails, a handsaw, and a bottle of carpenter's glue. In curious contrast to the rest of the shed, the workbench wasn't as dusty. Lauren paused to examine a sketch.

Outside the building, voices murmured.

"It's just a shed," came a petulant, velvety voice. "Let's go. If we don't hurry, we won't get back before the countdown."

"Hang on," came a male voice. "We need two more ping-pong balls."

Mari sighed. That last voice had sounded like Tony Rodriguez, with a definite Hispanic flavor to the words. Which probably meant the petulant voice belonged to Stefanie. Oh boy.

The door creaked open wider. Mari turned and found the glare of a flashlight in her face. She threw her arm up. "Hi," she said. "This shed's already occupied."

The flashlight beam lowered and Mari confirmed her guess. Yep. Tony and Stefanie.

"Oh, sorry," Tony said, ambling over as Lauren spun to face him. "Hi, Lauren. And hi again...what's your name?" he asked Mari, smiling.

"Her name's Mari. She's a sophomore," Stefanie cut in. She put an impatient hand on her hip. "So, you girls finding any ping-pong balls in here?"

"Three so far," Lauren said, throwing wary glances at both Tony and Stefanie.

Tony picked up one of the sketches on the workbench. Like the other sketches, it showed a triangle formed by a number of smaller triangles. The number of inner triangles varied from sketch to sketch, but the topmost inner triangle was always outlined darker. A three-dimensional, wooden triangle stood propped at the back of the workbench.

"Someone's creative," Tony said, putting down the sketch. "Are these yours, Stefanie?"

"No way," Stefanie said. "This isn't our property. This is Mr. Simpson's field. He let us use it for the treasure hunt, and he hid the balls for us." She pointed her flashlight under the workbench. "There's one you missed," she said to Mari and Lauren with smug satisfaction. "Can you get it for me, Tony-kins? It's in the left corner there."

"Sure." Tony dropped to his knees and crawled under the workbench.

"Watch out for spiders," Mari said, eyeing the murky space underneath. She didn't envy Tony's mission. And wow, he was certainly quick to obey. Stefanie cast her spell of enchantment upon the male world fast.

As Tony handed Stefanie the ball and brushed

16

cobwebs from his hair, the door creaked once again. Four swaths of light pinned the hesitant newcomer into motionlessness. "Hey, chill, people," a male voice said. "You're blinding me."

"Randall Stratton?" Stefanie said in scoffing disbelief. "What are you doing here?"

"Um, looking for ping-pong balls, of course," Randall said. "How's it going, Stef?"

Stefanie shrugged. "About done in here."

Mari watched Randall fling a venomous glare in Tony's direction. Clues of ulterior motives fell into place. She'd bet big bucks that Randall had been stalking Stefanie and Tony around the field. He probably feared this shed could be a place for Tony and Stefanie to make out, and wanted to interrupt. She wouldn't put it past him, as obsessed as he was about Stefanie.

"Mari, what are you and Lauren doing here?" Randall asked, waving his flashlight like an agitated baboon.

"We got here first," Mari said, "and then...." She trailed off, her mouth falling open. Her flashlight beam zipped upward where Randall's beam had briefly illumined an incredible sight. She laughed. "Whoa, look you guys. Jackpot!"

They looked up. Hanging from the ceiling was an old basket filled with ping-pong balls.

"Nice going, Mari," Tony said. "Here, I'll get those down." He grabbed the stool by the workbench, climbed onto it, and tugged at the basket. He wiggled it for a few moments and then yanked harder, setting it free, but a handful of balls shot out and bounced all over the room. Mari scurried to help gather the spilled balls. Tony jumped down, put the stool back, and snatched up golden balls with the rest of them.

A tinny beeping emitted from someone's watch, signaling the top of the hour.

Stefanie swore. "Oh, no. I can't believe it," she said, shining her flashlight at Randall's watch. "It's midnight, and we're missing the countdown."

Midnight. The year 2020 had begun--

No one had time to respond, because right then a thunderous booming shook the shed, rumbling and echoing around them. Mari ducked in a frightened reflex. Stefanie shrieked and latched onto the closest male, which happened to be Randall. The air around them grew brighter, glowing with a strange green light. A hissing, crackling noise filled the room.

"What the heck is going on?" Randall shouted, over the crackles and fading booms. "Stef, are you guys doing fireworks for New Year's?"

"No!" Stefanie yelled, her eyes wide.

Frozen with a ping-pong ball in her hand, Mari blinked. No, these weren't celebration sounds. Celebration sounds didn't make her skin crawl like this.

Lauren started for the half-open door, but Tony grabbed her arm. "Stay inside--it could be a weird electrical storm," he shouted, as the hissing magnified into a rushing howl.

The shelves and workbench began to reel and warp before Mari's eyes. A tremendous, magnetic-like force pulled on her arms and legs, trying to drag her toward the center of the shed. The ping-pong ball slipped from her hand. Her hair whipped across her face. The force increased, howling and raging like an uncontrolled storm. She dropped her flashlight with a bouncing clang and lunged for the edge of the workbench, trying to counteract the inward pull, her fingers scrabbling and her muscles taut.

Paper sketches of divided triangles swirled

demonically. Fluttering, suspended. Ping-pong balls skittered around the room, blown from the basket now discarded on the floor.

What was happening--a sudden freak cyclone, a twister? Had something nuclear or chemical been set off, causing the air to turn green? Was the world under alien attack?

Flashlight beams angled helter-skelter as the others struggled against the wind. Stefanie and Randall cringed in the middle of the room, wedged together. Their faces and clothing appeared greenish with the eerie light. Lauren clutched the knob of the open shed door, while Tony staggered and stumbled to his knees on the floor.

The howling, hissing crackle grew louder yet. Abandoning the doorknob, Lauren screamed and clapped her hands over her ears. She swayed and lurched, then spun across the room and rammed into Randall's shoulder.

Mari lost her grip on the edge of the workbench. She tried to brace herself against the pull, planting her feet and leaning away. It was too strong. The windy current built up, fast and faster, a dizzy whirlpool of motion that sucked her inward. She careened and jammed tight against Stefanie a split second after Tony rolled into Stefanie's legs. The howl rose to a frenzied roar, and everyone's confused cries became lost in the noise.

The green glow around them brightened with a sudden flash. A thick smell shot through the room, like something oily or rubbery burning--acrid, nauseating. At the same time, a blast of pain seared Mari's right forearm. She squeezed her eyes shut, and her scream became a tiny thread of sound, lost in the whirlwind of crashing noise and motion.

Chapter 2

Someone's ragged breathing stirred the hair by Mari's neck, and her right forearm throbbed. Her fingers and feet tingled like they'd been numb for a long time and re-awakened. Her body ached as though the strange howling wind had swept her a long, long distance. She opened her eyes slowly, afraid of what she might see.

Darkness. She saw mostly dim, shadowy darkness. The green light was gone. Only the pale beam of a single flashlight illuminated a jumble of arms and legs and torsos surrounding her on the ground. Someone moaned. She made out the straw-blonde of Lauren's hair, loose and tangled across someone's shirt, with the metallic glint of Stefanie's earrings beyond that. A dark arm shifted, lifting like a drowning person from a sea of tangled bodies.

The mass of straw-blonde hair moved. "Mari? Where are you?" Lauren's voice sounded muffled, raspy.

Mari coughed. "Here," she said, her own voice coming out clear, but thin and shaky. She eased into a sitting position, her shoulder and hip aching. "Are you okay?"

"I--I guess so. That hissing really messed with my hearing aids."

The stench of acrid burning still lingered in the air, and Mari fought an impulse to gag. With a grunt, she stretched to reach the flashlight. Other bodies and limbs began moving too, and groans of pain and confusion multiplied in the darkness. She grabbed the flashlight and swept it beyond the tangle of limbs. The darkness in that direction continued past the beam. She couldn't see the shed walls or the shelves or the workbench.

Freaky. Had the wind ripped the shed to pieces? Had it catapulted them far from the shed, to a different place? Her flashlight beam wobbled with the shaking of her hand. She sucked in a deep breath. Calm. She had to stay rational. Contrary to what her father claimed, she was more than a chicken-headed ninny filled with silly romance-novel ideas.

Blinking, she picked out shifting figures. Tony's shadowy self sat up, running his hands through his hair. Someone coughed, another person exhaled noisily and swore. A spiky-haired shape moved, revealing a second flashlight underneath him. Randall. He picked up the flashlight.

"Stef," he called out, scanning with the light. "Are you hurt?"

His light found Stefanie kneeling, her long hair swinging. "My arm hurts," she grumbled. "My leg too-- it was twisted and you were right on top of it."

"Oh, sorry."

"Whoa, what just happened?" Tony's voice sounded less self-assured. "Did someone throw us in a blender?"

Randall snorted. He stood and searched the darkness with his flashlight.

"Are there only two flashlights?" Lauren asked.

"I guess so," Mari said. She double-checked the ground with a sweep of her light.

Tony nudged Mari with his elbow. "I thought Lauren was deaf," he whispered.

"Hearing impaired," Mari corrected. "She hears some things with her hearing aids, and she reads lips. Great acoustics in here--wherever we are--but normally, she can only hear you if you're close to her or talking loudly."

"Oh."

"Hey, check this out," Randall said. "There are

21

walls here. Rock walls. They're above us and on three sides of us, and it looks like a tunnel goes off to the right. We're in a cave of some sort."

"What?" Stefanie screeched, scrambling to her feet. "That's impossible. Tony, I told you we should've gone back to the house instead of the shed!"

"Where *is* the shed?" Lauren said. "It couldn't have just disappeared."

Mari surveyed the murky shadows around them, and shuddered. She stood up and walked like a sleepwalker with rubbery legs, away from the others. Sure enough, about fifteen feet away, her beam revealed solid walls. She touched it to be certain. Yes, hard…as a rock. She swallowed, her mouth dry. This couldn't be happening. She had to be dreaming.

"Maybe the shed collapsed," Tony said, "and we fell through the flooring. We could be underground now."

"We would've felt that," Stefanie said scornfully. "Besides, how could we have fallen through when there's no opening above us now?"

"Whatever happened," Lauren said, "we can't stay in here. We'll have to follow that tunnel and see where it leads."

Mari shuddered again. Spiders could be scuttling around in this cave, or something larger could be lurking in the tunnel, like a bear. She ran her flashlight along the wall next to her. It seemed clear of cobwebs. Hard, dry rock surfaces, with nothing growing on them. Her beam caught the edge of a smoother area on the wall, and she frowned. It looked recessed, indented. She stepped over to examine it. The bottom dropped out of her stomach, and her lungs forgot how to breathe for a moment.

There, gouged into the wall as though it'd been etched with a giant laser, stretched a triangle three feet

22

tall, with narrow lines dividing it into five triangular parts. It looked like one of the sketches on the shed workbench.

"G-guys," she said. "Take a look at this."

Feet scuffled to gather beside her. Everyone gaped at the cave wall.

"Wow," Tony whispered in a wheezing exhale.

"So?" Stefanie said. "What is it, some sort of voodoo symbol?"

"Yeah, I don't get it," Randall said.

"Oh, you never saw the sketches in the shed," Tony said. "There were drawings of triangles like this all over your neighbor's workbench."

"This is weird," Lauren muttered.

Mari brushed one line of the huge triangle with her fingertips, trying to make sense of it all. The inner triangle she'd touched began to glow, green and eerie. Her fingers tingled. She flinched, jumping back with a cry.

Tony spouted an exclamation in Spanish, and Stefanie gasped.

The triangle glowed a second longer, then faded.

"What is this thing?" Mari cried.

Randall reached out toward the gouged markings. "Yeah, this is way beyond weird."

"No!" Mari grabbed his hand. "Leave it alone. Let's get out of here."

"Okay," Randall said, giving the triangle one last look. "We'll follow the tunnel and it should take us to the outside."

"Or to a grizzly bear," Stefanie grumbled.

"I'll protect you," Tony said, putting his arm around her shoulders and giving an encouraging squeeze. He grinned at Stefanie and didn't see the toxic look Randall threw his way. "Lead on, Captain Stratton," Tony said to Randall. "You and Mari have the flashlights."

Randall blew out an abrupt breath and set off toward their right. Tony and Stefanie fell into step behind him, and Mari followed with Lauren close by her side.

"It's getting lighter," Randall announced after a few curves.

No one answered him. Mari heard someone gulp. Their footsteps scraped and echoed over the rock flooring. What did it mean, that the tunnel led to a lighter place? If the tunnel ended up outdoors, there could be no sane reason for it to be getting lighter. Not at a few minutes after midnight.

She held her watch under her flashlight beam and frowned. Still midnight. Exactly. Somehow in that freaky green storm, her watch had stopped. The second hand twitched with a nervous tick, idling in one spot.

After a short while the tunnel widened, and they rounded a corner to find themselves at the mouth of the cave, where all was as bright as daylight.

"Dude," Randall said, slowing to a standstill. His flashlight arm dropped to his side.

Behind him, Stefanie clutched Tony's arm and went as pale as her hair color.

Mari halted so fast that Lauren bumped into her. Mari's words stuck in her brain, not even making it to her throat. Wrong and unreal, all of it. At her feet, a craggy mountainside worked its sloping way downward, giving way to impossibly emerald hills. Neon-pink flowers splashed the hills with perky, garish color. A golden road danced up and down over the hills, through the flowers, while the sun hovered at the edge of distant lavender hills.

Sunset?

Now she knew she had to be dreaming. In fact, once

24

when she was twelve, she'd had a dream with neon-pink flowers and a bright yellow road like this. Very memorable. It had turned into a hideous nightmare shortly afterwards.

"You've got to be kidding," Tony said, looking at his watch. "The sun can't be setting. Hey, my watch stopped at midnight."

"Mine too," Randall said.

Lauren shook her head. "Wow, were we unconscious for a while?"

"A whole day?" Stefanie scoffed, some pink coming back into her cheeks. "No way. And duh, this place looks like summer and not the dead of winter like it should be."

Mari clicked off her flashlight. Her eyes roamed the scenery. The sun sank into the curves of the hills like a melting glob of butter on a warm lavender plate. Over to her far right, a tangled forest lay. Its dense trees and foliage absorbed the evening's shadows, in contrast to the delicate leafy silhouettes of the trees on the hills by the sun. Within a few seconds after the sun vanished, the sky transformed. Almost white at the horizon, the sky rose and blossomed into light blue and then deeper blues, until at the very peak of the sky, the blues flared into a mysterious blue-violet. Everything looked rich. Saturated. Mari could almost taste the colors. Like the backdrop belonging to a fairy tale.

"Maxfield Parrish," she murmured, finding words at last.

Tony gave her the same perplexed look he'd been giving the landscape. "Uh, excuse me?"

"It's a painter I like," Mari said. "His landscapes have these same silhouetted trees and blended skies." She blinked watery eyes. Yes, like that beautiful old Maxfield Parrish picture she'd had hanging in her room in California, the one her grandmother had given her. The picture she'd lost when they'd moved here to Oregon in August.

If they were even in Oregon. It didn't exactly look like Oregon now.

"Is everyone having the same dream I'm having?" Randall wondered, his voice hollow. "Where's Stefanie's house? Where's the New Year's party, the shed, the ping-pong balls?"

"It doesn't feel like a dream," Lauren said. She plucked at her sweater sleeve. "For one thing, my arm hurts too much."

"So does mine," Stefanie grumbled, wriggling her arm out of her jacket sleeve. Then she shrieked, the shrillness of it slicing the calm of the landscape. A string of frantic swear words followed. She held out her arm, shaking. "My arm," she moaned. "Look at my arm!"

Tony looked, and snatched up his shirt sleeve. "*Ay!* It's on me, too."

"What?" Randall cried. He pushed up his sleeve as Mari and Lauren pushed up theirs.

Mari stared. There, across the inside of her right forearm, was a reddish-brown mark that looked like a tattoo or a colored welt. A few inches wide. Everyone-- all five of them--had the same mark, in the same place on their right arms.

Not only that, the mark was identical to the triangular design that had been gouged into the wall inside the cave.

Chapter 3

Mari gaped at her forearm, her head reeling. How in the world had the symbol from the cave ended up on their arms? The sketches in the shed had been variations of divided triangles, with varying numbers of sections, but this--this actually matched the cave's marking. The triangle shape, divided into five small triangles.

"We're *branded!*" Tony said in a hushed voice.

"But how, and why?" Lauren said. "Does it have anything to do with how we got here?"

"Who knows," Randall said, touching the mark on his arm. "Bizarre. It's like something from a science fiction movie."

Stefanie wailed, sinking to the ground, and began crying.

Mari bit her lip. She felt on the verge of doing the same thing, but not if Stefanie was doing it. Next to Mari, Randall shuffled and looked embarrassed at the sudden display of tears. Tony, however, crouched down to put his arm around Stefanie. He murmured some words into her ear, soft things Mari couldn't hear. His hand reached up to brush remnants of dancefloor glitter from Stefanie's hair.

Mari looked away. How gallant. Dark and handsome Tony, rushing to the aid of the gorgeous damsel in distress. Mari could bet Randall was kicking himself for his missed opportunity. Wow. More dramatic romance. She couldn't escape it.

"Do you think we should explore?" Lauren asked. Her face looked drawn, but determined. "We'll need to find a place to spend the night, plus food and water for the morning."

"Great idea," Randall said. "Maybe we can also find

someone who can help us, to tell us where we are."

"I am not spending the night in this crazy place!" Stefanie declared, dabbing at her eyes and making a hiccupping sob.

"I don't think we have a choice," Lauren said. "There's nothing in the cave that can help us." Her expression looked wistful as she watched Tony stroke Stefanie's hands.

"Yeah, I guess we have to," Mari said, walking toward the boulders and granite slabs that made up the craggy mountainside. She glanced back to see Tony speak something low to Stefanie, who sniffled and stood with him.

They picked their way over the rocks, making a careful downhill trail with the aid of their flashlights and an emerging moon. Soon the moon shone full upon them as they progressed, giving the rocks and surrounding landscape an iridescent, black-light appearance. A scattering of stars had emerged by the time they reached the first hill and the golden road that tumbled over it.

"Now what?" Tony asked, scanning the road both ways. "Follow the yellow brick road?"

"This isn't brick, Rodriguez," Stefanie growled.

Mari scuffed the shiny yellow dust of the road with the toe of her shoe. "Let's go right. I saw some sheep over that way before we climbed down the mountain. There might be people by the sheep."

"Okay," Randall said. "Uh, Tony, you want to lead with the flashlight for a while?"

"Aye, aye, Captain," Tony said with a salute.

Mari cracked a half-smile as Tony grabbed the flashlight and headed out, while Randall began walking beside Stefanie. No ulterior motives there, Randall Stratton. Oh no, none at all.

Lauren held out her hand in a silent offer to Mari, and Mari gave her the flashlight. They set off. Mari inhaled the sweet fragrance of the flowers scattered on the hills. Odd. It reminded her of the perfume her grandmother used to wear. Kind of a heady cross between lilac and honeysuckle. The scent began to fade as the hills leveled out into a wooded area where the flowers grew more sparse.

A zing of worry hit her as she watched the flashlight beams. Should they be conserving batteries, especially with the moonlight so bright and two flashlights not mandatory? Who knew how long they'd be in this place. She doubted they'd find a convenience store around the corner to purchase new batteries. It looked like countryside for miles.

They'd walked about twenty minutes when Lauren pointed to their right. "Look, there are the sheep."

Mari spotted a small group of sheep settling down for the evening in white clusters. Past the sheep, a little farther down the road, something square and white stood in front of some stubby trees. She peered into the gloom. It appeared to be a shabby little cottage. Yellow light radiated from the tiny windows.

"Cottage ahead," Tony said, as they walked closer. "Should we go knock?"

Before anyone could answer, the cottage door opened and out sprang a gnarled, white-bearded figure in tattered clothing. He bounded across the grass, waving stick-thin arms and opening his mouth in a wide grin. The few teeth he had glinted in the moonlight.

"Uh, you guys," Lauren said. "Incoming help."

"That's 'help'?" Tony asked. "Looks more like Rip Van Winkle."

"Or an escapee from a loony bin," Stefanie said, edging behind Randall.

29

Mari sidled closer to Lauren.

"Welcome, weary travelers!" the man called out in rusty, needle-thin voice. "You folk in need of food and water? A place to stay, or directions to yonder towns?" He gestured down the road with a bony hand, hobbling closer.

Randall found his voice first. "Yes, thanks, we need directions. And maybe a place to stay tonight."

"Ah," the thin man said, nodding his head as though it hung on a loose hinge, "you've likely come from Golmer then, eh? Well, come along, youngsters, come along." He scampered off toward the cottage, waving for them to follow.

"Do we *want* to stay there tonight?" Stefanie whisper-hissed. "He could be an axe murderer or a pervo."

"What, you see a motel nearby?" Tony said.

"Let's go," Lauren said, "but be careful, and stick together."

After a little hesitation, Mari started across the grass with the others.

"My name's Pod," the man said as he scurried along. "I'll set you up on the floor by the fire. Best place in my house, toasty warm. In the morning when you travel, stay left at the fork in the road, fifty yards hence. The road through the Fraghdom Forest may seem like a good shortcut to Permandy, but many a folk get lost or go plum crazy in there. Horrid things there, yessir. Evil. Hate to have that forest so near my place. But it's grown closer as the years go by, creeping almost right up into my backyard. I warn travelers whenever I can."

A shiver skidded down Mari's back. This Fraghdom Forest was evil, and nearby? That didn't sound comforting. She looked fifty feet beyond the cottage and a few apple trees, and saw a black tangle rising up.

That must be it. The Fraghdom Forest. It looked like the same forest she'd seen from the cave opening, absorbing shadows like something alive and ravenous.

Pod scurried into the cottage, and they followed him. Dried herbs hung from the ceiling along with iron pots and ladles. Randall ducked, missing a big pot by an inch. A pair of trousers dried by the fire, sending the smell of steaming cloth into the air. The pungent aromas of dillweed and honeycomb mingled with the wood smoke of the fire. A candle burned in a lantern on the table. The whole cottage appeared primitive and old-fashioned, from the rickety ladder perched by the loft, to the stone fireplace and the cracked butter churn.

Pod bustled around, gathering thick woolen blankets for the floor.

"Funky place," Randall murmured.

Mari elbowed him into more polite quietness. She'd never been a fan of medieval decor and inconveniences either, but they didn't have to be rude about it. They really didn't have a choice about their lodgings.

"Hot flatcakes in the morning," Pod rattled on. "Maybe some fresh blackberries too, if I get my old bones out to the patch and pick 'em early--" He halted and straightened, a blanket hanging from his hand. "Hush! What's that?" he said.

The alarm in the old man's voice froze them all into abrupt silence.

Mari listened. Far off, a distant thudding reached her ears. It pounded out rhythmically, a frenzied drumbeat of shuddering sound.

"Horses!" Pod said, his eyes wild. "I bet it's them confounded Shifters--hurry out back, all of you."

They obeyed the urgency of Pod's command, fleeing with the old man out a narrow back door, past a pair of goats in a pen, and across a grassy slope. Mari's

31

heartbeat thundered in her ears with the approaching horses' hooves. The sound rumbled, unnaturally loud and echoing. She ran with the others past stubby apple trees, until she realized that Pod had stopped at the trees and was shooing them straight toward the edge of the Fraghdom Forest.

"Go on," Pod said. "Hide, quick! I must get back to the cottage."

"Hide in this forest?" Stefanie cried. "But I thought you said--"

"It's safer than those Shifters if you only go in a few feet. Now hurry, and don't come out until I tell you it's safe."

Breathless, Mari reached the murkiness of the forest growth. Tony grabbed Stefanie's hand and pulled her into the shadows. Randall and Lauren followed. A clammy chill washed over Mari's body as she entered the forest, making her feel as though she'd plunged into a pool of ice water.

Lauren clutched Mari's arm and gave a startled gasp.

"Whoa," Tony yelped. "It's a freezing graveyard in here."

Unnerved further, Mari slugged him in the shoulder.

"Hey! What was that for--"

"Shhh," Randall ordered. "The horses are stopping at the cottage."

Mari peered from behind the cover of the trees, her legs trembling. Five figures in great flapping black cloaks swung down from their horses. They pounced upon the ground like malevolent ravens and strode toward the front of the cottage. The cottage blocked her view after that. She heard distant harsh voices, and jerked as a shattering crash splintered the air.

Who were these Shifters? Was Pod going to be all

right?

Tension huddled them closer together. Behind Mari's back, the forest crawled up with tangible fingers, pressing fear into her spine. Something skittered across her feet, and she sucked in a sharp breath. That was no freaking leaf. She clamped her teeth together to prevent a scream.

Another crash came from the cottage. She heard shouting, harsh and demanding, though she couldn't make out the words

More skittering happened by Mari's feet. This time, the motion of many legs settled upon her shoe, and she felt a tugging at the hem of her jeans. After a bit of scrabbling the multiple legs worked their way under her hem. Then, in a few seconds, the legs plucked at her sock. Her eyes squeezed closed. A thin moan of terror escaped her lips.

Whatever evil creature or big insect lurked down there, it was trying to get past her sock to her bare ankle. She twitched her leg, trying to fling whatever it was off. It tightened around her sock and hung on.

Behind her, Randall clamped a quieting hand on her shoulder. The black-cloaked figures swept from the back of the cottage, scattering with lanterns to search behind bushes and the apple trees. The goats bleated like frightened children. The dim figure of Pod appeared beside the cottage, shaking his gnarled hands.

"I told you, good sirs," Pod said, his voice quavering, "I was merely airing my extra woolens. There are no visitors here."

The Shifters paid him no heed. One cloaked figure tromped the hillside less than fifteen feet away. His lantern swung by, glowing like a giant's eye in the darkness. At Mari's feet, the horrible tiny tugging at her sock continued. Her back and underarms stung with nervous sweat. Quiet! She couldn't make any noise now. She twitched her leg again, but the creature clung to her.

Standing on her right, Tony glanced from her to the nearby Shifter, then back to her.

The unseen poking legs resumed their work at her feet. She looked down--and wished to the stars she hadn't. Illumined by streaks of moonlight, she saw a hairy dark shape perched on top of her right shoe, the body of it four or five inches across. Its pointed legs reached under her jeans, scraping at her sock.

It was a huge, *huge* spider.

The ghastly creature clawed her sock away from her ankle. She felt a sudden fluttering on her skin, then a sharp prick. Her scream rose from the very core of her soul, sucked up past her lungs, ripped from her throat by fists of pure terror.

Chapter 4

The scream lasted only a second. Tony's hand shot up and clamped over Mari's mouth, smothering most of the sound. Muffled bits of it escaped around his fingers. At the same time, he gave a savage kick to the grotesque spider on her foot. Its plump black shape shot away, crashing into the bushes eight feet to their left.

The nearby Shifter jerked his head up. He lifted his lantern, peering into the forest.

Another Shifter moved closer. "Did you see something, Zander?" he demanded.

"Not really," Zander said. "I heard noises. A short scream and a crash. You want to investigate?"

"Not in there," the second Shifter said. "Are you insane? Not with vampire spiders and howling shadows prowling around, plus acid mushrooms and other unmentionables."

"Yeah." Zander lowered his lantern. "I doubt anyone's in there. I probably heard a howling shadow."

In the forest, Tony's hand eased from Mari's mouth. Mari trembled and darted a fearful glance at her feet. Nothing there now. She swallowed, feeling faint. Vampire spiders, the Shifter had said? She'd just been bitten by a *vampire spider?* And what the heck-- howling shadows and acid mushrooms? She'd read about those in a science fiction novel Randall had left lying around the house a few years ago. They'd given her recurring nightmares, and after that she'd sworn off science fiction and stuck to adventure and romance novels.

Creepy. How could those things be here, actually existing someplace?

A harsh, grating voice shouted across the grass. "Zander! Markus! You finding anything over there?"

"Nothing, Bierce," Zander called. "All clear, sir."

Bierce's tall form stood like a daunting black pillar in the moonlight. "All right, old man," he said to Pod, "I don't know where you've hidden or sent the newcomers, but you'll pay for not cooperating." He gave a shout and gestured toward the cottage. "Burn it down!"

The raven-like forms of the other Shifters obeyed, converging upon the cottage and lighting the thatched roof. Flames leaped and began to devour the roofing, turning it into a livid torch.

Pod cried out, moaning and sinking to his knees in the grass. The two goats nearby bawled and kicked, terrified by the crackling heat. Pod leaped into action and hobbled to them, grabbing a length of rope and herding them from their pen.

The five Shifters mounted their horses with disdainful sweeps of their cloaks. They galloped off with fading shouts of plans to conduct a search for newcomers in Golmer.

When the Shifters could no longer be seen and the sounds of thundering hoofs had receded, Pod called out in a weary voice. "All right, youngsters, it's safe to come out now."

Mari hurried from the Fraghdom Forest with the others. A few feet out, she stumbled, her spider-bitten ankle throbbing. Her head swam. Randall caught her arm.

"Hey, sis," he said. "You okay? Why'd you scream in there?"

Mari wilted against Randall. "It bit me--it bit me on the ankle," was all she could manage to say. Oh no. She'd die for sure. A spider that huge had to be majorly poisonous.

"Big ugly spider," Tony added. "Five inches wide. I kicked it."

"Oh, disgusting. I wondered what you'd kicked." Lauren said.

"Gross!" Stefanie said with a shudder. "I'm never going in that forest again."

"My ankle hurts," Mari said, limping with Randall toward Pod.

Pod knelt beside his goats, tears streaming down his face. Lauren walked over and put her hand on his bony shoulder. "I'm sorry," she said, gazing with him at his still-burning home. "This happened because of us."

Shaking his head, Pod tied the goats together and stood to loop the other end of the rope around an apple tree. "Don't take the blame, miss. It's them fool Shifters' fault. Them and their obsession to find some special kind of newcomers. Zealous fanatics, the whole lot of them."

"Why do they want newcomers?" Tony asked.

Pod shrugged. "Don't rightly know. I reckon newcomers figure into their crackpot beliefs some way or another. I don't think they've ever found any around here, but they keep looking."

"Well, thanks for hiding us," Lauren said

Mari's vision began to go fuzzy. "Randall, I need to sit."

As Randall helped her sit on the grass, Pod bobbled over. "Trouble in the forest, young lady? Spider or a zillipede, maybe?"

"Spider. It bit me here," Mari said, taking off her shoe and pushing her sock down. She wasn't even going to ask what a zillipede was, though the word sounded disturbingly familiar. Randall took her flashlight and turned it on, aiming it at her ankle. A smear of blood showed next to her ankle bone, along with a wicked set of puncture marks.

"Ah, a bit puffy and red," Pod said. "From the juices

in their mouths. Unless it gets infected, that'll fade in a few days. Those spiders aren't poisonous. They're bloodsuckers, taking out more than they put in."

Profound relief washed over Mari, leaving her trembling with spent adrenaline.

"Sorry you got bit, miss," Pod said. "Usually them critters stay farther inside the forest. Must've been a stray one on the fringes." He gave a wary nod at their flashlights. "Never seen them light cylinders before. Nor your style of footwear or clothing. Reckon you might be the kind of newcomers the Shifters are looking for, all right." He gave a sigh and threw a glance at the smoldering skeletal remains of his cottage. "Come with me, youngsters. We'll sleep in the field by the sheep, and you can be on your way come morning."

A trilling chirrup of a bird awakened Mari. Her surroundings invaded her mind in gradual stages. Her ankle, throbbing and aching. The weedy, damp smell of grass blades. Stiffness in her shoulder and hip where she lay on the ground. Her eyes opened, and she saw the textured sight of Lauren's purple sweater and the thick mass of her straw-blonde hair. A goat bleated, standing nearby.

Dang. Still stuck in this strange place. Wherever "this place" was. It had all the signs of a twisted dream, yet with all the heightened senses and stark feelings of reality. Was she really dead or in a coma, and her brain lived on in some sort of demented half-life?

She sat up. A few feet away, Tony rubbed sleep from his dark-lashed eyes and naturally tanned face. She stared as he raked fingers through his hair and it fell into perfect disarray. She didn't know how some guys could do that. He looked awesome, even after a night of sleeping on the hard ground, only half-awake, and wearing a wrinkled shirt.

Tony looked at her and winked. His teeth flashed in a quick grin. "Buenos días, señorita bonita," he said, low. "Sleep okay?"

"Uh, as well as I could, considering," Mari said with a faltering smile. She could guess at most of what he'd said, but "bonita" wasn't in her mental Spanish-English dictionary. Trying to smooth her hair, she rose to her feet as the others began waking and shifting. A small group of sheep nibbled grass with the goats to their left, and way off to their right, Pod's stringy figure poked among the wreckage of his home. The stone fireplace of the former cottage stood like a blackened tombstone in the smoldering ruins.

Randall yawned, stretched, and looked around. His previously spiked hair lay flat on one side, as well as the back. So much for flawless perfection. "No public restrooms or outhouses here, I assume," he said, "so bushes will have to do."

"Easy for you to say," Stefanie said with a sniff, flicking her hair behind her shoulders as she stood up.

Lauren pointed to a line of bushes on the opposite side of the road. "Girls on that side of the road," she announced. "Boys, stay here."

Sighing, Mari trudged across the road to the gender-appropriate bushes. Yes, indoor plumbing and toilet paper definitely qualified as two of mankind's better inventions. She'd get no shower today, either. What a drag. The things a person took for granted in normal everyday life.

After accomplishing those rustic duties, they reassembled as Pod returned with assorted salvaged pots and other metal items from the cottage. They consumed a breakfast of goat's milk and apples, and washed off Mari's spider bite with water from an adjacent creek.

Pod scrunched his face into a thoughtful pucker as Mari put her sock and shoe back on. "Today I'm off to Golmer," he said. "My sister will take me and the critters in for a spell. You youngsters traveling on to Permandy?"

Randall shrugged, looking around at everyone. "I guess so."

"Where else?" Lauren said, also shrugging.

Stefanie's mascara-smudged eyes puddled up with emotion. She looked away, blinking, and her hand slipped into Tony's.

"Well," Pod said, "Never been to Permandy myself, but best of luck to you on your journey."

They said farewell to Pod and started down the glittery yellow road. Mari looked back to see Pod wave and give a gaping grin. Heeding his advice of the evening before, they angled left at the fork in the road. Mari shivered as she glanced at the right fork. The peppy golden path veered straight for the Fraghdom Forest, penetrating the shroud of darkness for a short stretch before becoming swallowed up by its shadows.

The morning dragged on as they walked. Warm summer rays beamed down from the cloudless sky, and soon Stefanie shed her jacket, giving it to Tony to hold. Randall, the only other possessor of a jacket, shed his too. After a while they reached the top of a hill and looked down upon a quaint village teeming with livestock and people dressed in peasant-type clothing.

Mari squinted up at the sun. Not quite directly overhead, so it must be late morning. They'd walked two or three hours. Her ankle throbbed worse now. She hoped it wouldn't get infected.

"Remind me again why we're going to this town," Stefanie said, a pout lacing her voice. "Are we all going to rent cottages and get peasant jobs, since we'll be stuck in this psycho place for the rest of our lives?"

"We could use some food," Tony said. "And someone might know how we can get back to your house."

Randall nodded. "Yeah. Keep your ears open for anything to do with Shifters or these weird triangle marks."

"Didn't that old guy say we're dressed differently from most people?" Lauren asked. "If everyone dresses like him, it's going to be obvious we're newcomers."

"Who cares?" Stefanie said. "Pod only talked about Shifters being fanatics about strangers."

Mari glanced at Lauren with a thoughtful frown. That "old guy"? Hadn't Lauren heard Pod say his name? Perhaps not. He'd been hobbling toward his cottage when he'd introduced himself. She should never assume Lauren heard everything they heard, and try to keep her updated.

They resumed their hike, winding their way down to the village. Cottages with pens holding nonchalantly chewing goats and rotund pink pigs dotted the fields. Sheep also grazed. Small vegetable gardens accompanied most cottages. Children hoed, fed animals, and carried buckets of water alongside the adults. A woman bellowed an objection as two dirt-smudged girls dropped their hoes with metallic twangs, and ran after Mari and the others.

Tony looked over his shoulder as three more children joined the first two. Their upturned faces were curious and their eyes round. "Uh, guys," he said, "we seem to be attracting a fan club."

"Can't do much about that," Lauren said.

The children giggled and whispered behind their hands. One little girl with matted hair pointed to

Stefanie's bright red jacket draped over Tony's arm, and chirped, "Look! It's shiny."

"Ugh," Stefanie said, her lip curling. "I hope these kids don't have lice."

Mari's stomach formed a queasy knot around her measly apple-and-goat-milk breakfast. She had a feeling they'd be wasting their time in this town. No information or help, she'd bet. Argh, and the *smell*, here in the valley. Not only did the children reek like the animals and dirty ground they tended, but the air had a kind of heavy, charcoal smell to it, sticking to the insides of her nostrils like old hamburger grease.

They approached a bustling village area that looked like an outdoor farmer's market, with metal cookware and earthen pots on wooden tables, rows of vegetables in shades of green and yellow and orange, and hunks of rough-woven cloth displayed in uneven stacks. The merchants, as well as the shopping townsfolk, looked up as Mari and the others passed, their suspicious stares following Mari's group and their dirty parade of children. A number of people joined the children to walk alongside. Others made curious flicking motions with one hand across their face and then back over the opposite shoulder.

"See the evil witches," one woman in a dingy apron hissed. "They come to cast spells."

"Fetch the Magistrate!" another woman called.

"Quick, use the sign-against-evil," a fat, bearded man said, making the flicking motion across his face and shoulder.

Randall frowned. "Blast it all. They think we're witches."

"Because of our clothes?" Lauren said.

"I think so," Mari said.

Stefanie gave a nervous squeal. "Oh no, they're

gonna burn us at the stake or something. I knew we shouldn't have come to this stupid little hick town. Whose idea was this, anyway?"

A burly man with a pitchfork appeared in the road, blocking their path. They halted. The number of children and townspeople had grown to a sizeable crowd by this time, and stopped in a restless swarm around them.

"Where you folk from?" the burly man demanded. "We don't take kindly to outsiders here in Permandy."

Mari tried to swallow, but was unable. She couldn't find her voice, either. Luckily, Randall found his.

"Today we've walked from, uh, near Golmer," Randall said.

The man spat on the ground. "Hogswallow. Been to Golmer once or twice, myself. I didn't see nothin' close to the likes of what y'all are wearing there."

The crowd murmured, sounding as agitated as a disturbed hornet's nest.

"Well, we weren't actually in Golmer," Tony said. "Originally we came from much farther away than that, and people in our village always wear clothes like this. We can't help it if yours don't."

"Yeah, get over it," Stefanie snapped.

Mari resisted an urge to reach back and smack Stefanie. It wouldn't help them at all in this situation if they were rude.

The burly man glared at Stefanie, then at all of them in turn. "What's your business here in Permandy?" he growled.

"We'd like some food," Tony said. "Then we'll be on our way."

The burly man snorted. "No charity. With outsiders, we only trade in coins or goods."

"Okay," Randall said, pulling out a large handful of

change from his jeans pocket. "Is this enough buy sausage or a loaf of bread or something?"

Mari groaned. Oh no, modern money. Bad move.

The burly man inched forward to peer at the coins. He jerked back. "Doesn't look like money I've ever seen. What're you trying to pull?"

"Witch money!" someone from the crowd yelled. "Don't take it, it's cursed."

"It'll turn you into a mud-toad or a chicken," a shrill voice called.

"Let's toss these outsiders into the Pit," the burly man snarled. He moved nearer with a menacing expression, brandishing his pitchfork.

The crowd pressed inward with him, emboldened by the burly man's advance. Cries of "In the pit!" rang out.

Mari bumped into Stefanie as she backed up. Stefanie latched onto Tony's arm. Tony threw a frantic look around them, while Lauren chewed her lip and Randall quickly re-pocketed his coins. Anything called the Pit couldn't be good. They were doomed.

The burly man took another step closer, egged on by the peasants. Then a reedy voice cut through the mumblings and threats of the crowd.

"What seems to be the problem here?"

The burly man lowered his pitchfork and turned as a stout, balding figure plowed through the parting crowd. Six armored soldiers with swords accompanied the stout man.

"Uh, we've got some possibly dangerous outsiders here, Mr. Magistrate, sir," the burly man said. "These strangers say they're from beyond Golmer."

"Do they, now." The Magistrate halted and scrutinized the five of them, hands on his hips. His gaze snagged on Tony and Lauren. "You two," he said, pointing. "What are those tools you're carrying? Or are they weapons?"

Tony held out his flashlight. "Uh, it's a fancy lantern, Mr. Magistrate. It makes light."

"Very curious." The Magistrate took Tony's flashlight, as well as Lauren's, his wiry eyebrows rising in fascination as he examined them. Mari swapped a concerned look with Lauren. Would they get the flashlights back?

"In the Pit!" the fat, bearded man yelled.

"Nonsense," the Magistrate said with irritation. "The Pit is reserved for those who have committed heinous crimes against the village. I've seen no evidence that these young folk have done anything of the sort."

"They have witch money, yer Honor!" someone yelled.

"Let's see it," the Magistrate ordered.

Randall pulled out his change again, and the Magistrate confiscated that, too.

"Don't give him anything else," Stefanie whispered. "He's taking all our stuff."

A woman with a ruddy face shook a fleshy arm at Lauren. "Take a gander at that gal's ears, yer Honor-- those are witch contraptions, for certain."

People in the crowd looked and gasped.

The Magistrate's eyebrows lowered into a concerned frown. "What are those strange fleshy pebbles in your ears, girl?"

Lauren took out one of her hearing aids, causing a brief stampede backward as the peasants reacted. She held it out toward the Magistrate. "It's not a pebble. It's a hearing aid. It makes sounds louder and helps me hear things better."

"Aha, I knew it," the ruddy-faced woman crowed.

"It helps her listen--to spy on other folk. Devil's ears, black magic!"

"That's silly," Lauren said, matching the Magistrate's dark frown as she replaced her hearing aid. "We're not witches and there's no such thing as black magic. We've traveled from a place that has different things from what you have, that's all."

The Magistrate's stout figure straightened into a rigid line. "Are you Shifters, then?" he demanded. "Have you brought your clothing and strange devices from other dimensions or landscapes?"

Mari felt her mouth fall open. Other *dimensions?* What in the--

"No way, we're not Shifters," Randall assured the Magistrate. "They're harsh. They burned down a nice old man's cottage."

"That sounds like them," the Magistrate said, almost to himself. He cleared his throat and raised his arm to silence the muttering crowd. "Let's put an end to this nonsense. Newcomers, are you well, and fit?"

"Definitely," Tony said. He gestured toward Mari. "Except Mari's limping a little. She got bitten by a vampire spider last night."

"Ah, I see," the Magistrate said with a nod, suddenly all business. He set the soldiers into motion with a flick of his free hand. "Guards, take the boys to the mines. Two of you lock the witch-girl in an Isolation cell. The other blonde goes to the workhouse, and take the Mari girl to the Haven for healing before going to the workhouse."

"No!" Stefanie cried. "You can't do that. We need a trial--and a lawyer."

"Please, sir, we can't be separated," Randall said to the Magistrate.

The Magistrate spun and strode away, taking the

flashlights and coins with him. Two stern-faced soldiers flanked Randall and Tony, two more approached Lauren, and a grizzled-looking one marched up to Stefanie. The sixth soldier divided Mari from the others with a terse movement of his sword. The sun glinted with a chilling flash upon the metal surface. Mari cringed.

The crowd of peasants roared approval of the Magistrate's judgments, clenching their hands into exultant, raised fists.

Chapter 5

The two soldiers in charge of Lauren bustled her away down a side street, through a gap in the crowd. Stefanie's cries and desperate swearing faded as she was taken in the opposite direction. Mari's soldier marched her along behind Randall and Tony and their guards, until they reached a sparser section of town. The stench of greasy charcoal grew stronger.

Randall threw Mari a concerned look as his group veered left toward a crude barracks-type building next to a hillside. Soot-covered workers emerged from a stony outcropping in the hillside, piling huge black rocks into carts. The mines.

"We'll all get back together somehow, don't worry!" Randall called to her.

Mari clenched her teeth. What made Randall so sure of that? It looked hopeless to her. He and Tony getting assigned to the mines, and Stefanie the workhouse. And poor Lauren, sentenced to an Isolation cell--how horrid. They'd never be able to figure out what was going on and get back to the real world, if they were all prisoners or slaves here in Permandy.

The real world...what had the Magistrate meant, when he'd asked if their clothing and devices had come from other dimensions or landscapes? Had the triangular markings somehow transported her and the others into another *dimension* at the stroke of midnight? Oh. No. Way. That was so far-fetched it was laughable.

And yet, what other explanation was there?

The soldier tromped and clanked beside her until they reached the outskirts of town. Leaving the golden road, he steered her onto a rutted dirt road lined with trees.

"Ouch, can we slow down a little?" Mari asked the

soldier. "My ankle is killing me."

The soldier didn't answer, but reduced the pace a little.

After a few minutes, a large gray building became visible. It stretched out in boxy sections over the fields like a stiff hand. A wrought-iron fence with a locked gate surrounded it.

The Haven, she assumed. It looked more like a prison.

When they arrived at the gated entrance of the wrought-iron fence, the soldier rang a large bell hung on a post. Engraved, somber letters on the gate announced, "The Haven of Peaceful Solitude and Rest." Mari blinked. Well, that didn't sound too bad.

Before the clanging echoes of the bell had faded away, a slim male figure in a hooded brown monk's robe darted from a shelter on the other side of the fence and unlocked the gate.

"The Magistrate sent this one," the soldier drawled. "Outsider. Bitten by a vampire spider, staying 'til she heals. The workhouse will fetch her in three days."

The gatekeeper nodded, waiting with an air of eternal patience while Mari hobbled through the gate. Mari threw a nervous glance at the tall bars of the gate as it closed behind her with a clank of solid finality. She trailed the gatekeeper across a cobbled courtyard and entered the Haven.

In an undecorated entryway, the gatekeeper knocked upon a dark brown door marked with the letter "H." The door opened to a woman in a white robe, her gray hair pulled into such a tight bun that her eyebrows angled upward. It gave her a look of perpetual, haughty surprise.

The gatekeeper repeated the soldier's instructions, and left.

"I am Headmistress," the woman said to Mari, her voice as stiff as her posture. "Welcome. There are five wings here at the Haven. First is the nursing area where we will tend your bite. Second is the music room, third is the library, fourth is the gardens. The fifth is the living quarters where you will eat, bathe, and sleep."

"Okay," Mari said, feeling subdued. She followed the Headmistress to the nursing area, where a white-robed nurse washed her ankle and smeared it with a sticky ointment. She was instructed to return twice a day, for the next three days. Afterwards the Headmistress gave her a quick tour and then showed her to a small room with a wooden cot, one blanket, and a lantern. A round skylight in the ceiling let in filtered sun. A brown monk's robe like the gatekeeper's lay on the cot, with a pair of leathery shoes underneath.

The Headmistress gave a curt nod toward the cot. "While inside the Haven, you are required to wear the robe and footwear provided. Talking with other inhabitants is permitted as long as it's minimal." She tapped a long finger at a number carved into the door. "Your identification number is 131199. It is not advised, but if you wish to leave the Haven for a brief period of time during the day, this is the number you will recite at the gate to regain access. And remember, the ten o'clock curfew in Permandy is strictly enforced, so return prior to that time. Is all this clear?"

"Yes," Mari said, feeling lightheaded from the Headmistress' barrage of words.

"Then I will leave you. You may change and seek out your midday meal."

"Thanks," Mari whispered. She sank onto her cot as the door closed, clutching the coarse material of the robe. A curfew. Oh, no. No, no, *no*. The curfew had better not mean what she thought it meant. That hideous nightmare she'd had when she was twelve had started out with those frilly neon-pink flowers on an emerald green hillside. In the dream she'd hiked into a primitive-looking town, which had possessed a strict ten o'clock curfew. The penalty for breaking curfew had been deadly and horrifying.

But hold on. She had to be panicking for nothing--it would be impossible to have that childhood nightmare come true here in Permandy. Her empty stomach had to be short-circuiting the logic of her brain. She needed food, something to eat. If her father were here, he'd be shaking his head right about now, chiding her for being an unthinking and emotional female.

She changed into the monk's robe and slipper-like shoes, and hurried to the food area, passing a number of robed inhabitants. Most people kept their eyes cast down, their faces almost hidden by their hoods. About a dozen people occupied the meal room. At a wooden table spread with an array of simple food, Mari gathered a mug of milk, a plump roll filled with meat, and a peach. She sat on an empty bench to eat. The milk tasted too strong and thick, like fresh raw milk, and the meat roll tasted suspiciously like lamb. Not caring, she ate in ravenous gulps and bites.

A sense of guilt pressed upon her as she finished, wiping sweet peach juice from her chin. Were Randall, Lauren, Tony, and Stefanie getting anything to eat? She shuddered. The mines had looked like hard work. All those heavy rocks. The idea of going to a workhouse didn't sound much better--and in three days that would be her fate, too.

All of them were trapped now, except for her. Odd that the Haven would let her wander outside the gates, but it meant that her next three days here might be their only hope for escape and getting crucial information.

51

She pulled her robe tighter around her. A shiver of apprehension ran down her back. Only three days, and what could she do if she left the Haven? She didn't want to act like a stereotypically weak female, but it seemed really dangerous out there. She might be recognized, and even if she wasn't, who knew what other terrible things lurked in this freaky dimensional world. What if she went to the workhouse to help Stefanie escape, and she got locked up early? She didn't have a key to release Lauren from a probably locked cell, and soldiers might be guarding Randall and Tony. And where, exactly, were the Isolation cells and the workhouse?

She stood up with a groan. If someone else had gotten bitten by the vampire spider, she wouldn't have to be making this decision. Why her? Talk about rotten luck. Randall and Lauren were more the take-charge, level-headed kind. Adventurous and brave. They should be the ones sitting here at the Haven with this chance to be valiant and rescue everyone.

Not her.

She returned her mug to the food area and wandered down the hall. Maybe she'd stay inside and take it easy today. She could check out the library wing, which sounded interesting. If she went outside too soon, her spider bite might get infected. That was logical, right? She'd be of no use to anyone if she got sick or died in this forsaken town.

Besides, the library might have books with information on the strange triangles or the Shifters. A history of the town of Permandy, or some such book.

It was settled. Destination: the library.

The library wing lay in the center of the five wings. The huge room was narrow but very long, the shelves divided by a central row of wooden tables. A few robed figures sat huddled over books at the tables, some wearing hoods, some not. Mari meandered to the right and scanned a few titles on the shelves. *A Promise for All Time. Love Knows No Boundaries. The Heart's Folly.* Oh. She'd stumbled upon the romance novel section of the library. Not really what she wanted to read right now. Her mind still stung from the freeze-frame image of Brad swimming as a symbiotic unit with Susan DeBarge in the Anders' pool.

What other fiction did they have? Maybe this side of the room held fiction, and the other side nonfiction. She skipped a number of rows and stopped to read more titles. *Renaissance of the Heart. Forever Love.* She put her hands on her hips.

Wow, too weird. This entire half of the room seemed to be stocked with romance novels. She crossed the room to check out the left side. Her head began to spin with confused disbelief as she roamed the left aisles. Here on the left side, the books all seemed to be adventure novels--forages into exotic lands, flights into magical fantasy worlds, and journeys into unknown realms.

How could this library hold only her favorite two kinds of books, and no others?

Shaking her head, she grabbed an adventure book. She would read it later. She meandered back to the middle of the room, surveying the robed readers at the tables. Since this library didn't contain nonfiction or any helpful information, maybe she could get some clues from these people.

Mari hovered by a wide woman reading *The Dragons of Sherlina*. "Hi," she said. "That looks like a good book."

"Yeah," the woman said with a grunt, and settled into her reading again.

Okay. Not the talkative type. Maybe the library

wasn't the best place to try to talk with someone, anyway. Mari strolled back to her room, dumped her book there, and wandered into the garden wing. The courtyard-like wing was roofless, open to the outside air and sky. She walked down the colorful paths, inhaling. The fruity fragrance of the blooming flowers covered the thick, greasy smell of the mines nearby. That in itself was a good thing.

A thin, lone woman who appeared to be in her early twenties sat on a bench with eyes closed, lifting her face to the sun. Her hood was down. She looked fragile and tired.

Mari began to walk by, but the woman opened her eyes.

"Hello," the woman said. "I'm Lynia. Are you new?"

"Yes," Mari said. Lynia patted the bench, and Mari sat.

"What're you in for?" Lynia asked. "I'm hiding from my husband. He's too heavy-handed with the strap for my liking. I come as often as the Haven allows, which is three days every moon's cycle."

"That's sad," Mari said, aghast. It seemed the Haven also functioned as a shelter for battered women. "I'm here three days for a vampire spider bite." She wasn't going to say anything about being a newcomer. In Permandy, that seemed to be an unpopular subject.

Lynia nodded. "I've heard of those spiders. Big and ugly, but mostly they stay in the Fraghdom Forest. Did you happen upon a stray one on the outskirts of town?"

"No," Mari said, sensing a perfect opening to gain some information. "I was actually inside the edge of the Forest, hiding from Shifters."

"Shifters." Lynia made a sour face. "Now there's a cruel group. Everyone's afraid of the Shifters. Afraid not to obey them, afraid of their strange exploding weapons. They point those weapons, and bam!--smoke comes out and folk are dead upon the ground. So much blood. Have you seen the Shifters use those weapons?"

"No, I haven't." Mari assumed Lynia meant guns. But how would Shifters come into possession of guns in this primitive setting? Even the Magistrate's soldiers had swords rather than guns.

"Unfortunately," Lynia added, "at this time of year the Shifters roam around more than they usually do."

This time of year. Around New Year's Eve?

"What do the Shifters want?" Mari asked.

Lynia shrugged. "They're looking for newcomers, folk who come from a fantasy place they call the Mainworld. I reckon they think all strangers who travel this time of year are Mainworlders."

"Is the Mainworld a different dimension?" Mari asked, her voice almost a whisper.

"So the Shifters say. That's their sole purpose in life, to capture a newcomer and hitch a wondrous ride to the blessed Mainworld." Lynia gave a dry laugh. "Such utter rot."

Mari had to remind herself to breathe. Was the real world what the Shifters called the Mainworld? If so, it sounded like there might be some way to get back to it.

Lynia smoothed the knees of her robe. "My, but this is an awful discussion. We should dwell on more pleasant or relaxing things. Have you visited the music wing yet?"

"No, I haven't," Mari admitted, reluctant to leave the subject of Shifters.

"Then you should. Would you like to see it now?"

"All right," Mari said. She followed Lynia's thin figure from the gardens and past the library to the music wing. Faint swirling sounds filtered into her ears as

Lynia opened an outer door. They stood in an entryway which contained three labeled doors.

"Each door has different music, for different moods," Lynia said. "Calming, Joyous, and Invigorating. Try them and see which one you like. It works best when you experience it alone, so I'll leave you to try it out."

"Thanks," Mari said. "See you later, maybe."

Lynia nodded and exited while Mari felt herself being drawn to the middle door, the one labeled Joyous. She turned the knob and slipped inside. A glorious Maxfield Parrish sky stretched out, painted on the walls and ceiling. The magic stream of the music flowed around her, throwing her soul sky high, the pulsing beat calling for her feet to move. No voices accompanied the music, only rhythm and breathtaking sounds.

Three other brown-robed figures danced in the room. They swayed by themselves, absorbed in the music.

Mari spun, her emotions soaring. She discovered the heartbeat of the room and stepped to mimic it. Looking down, she smiled. The floor appeared almost liquid, as deep green as golf course grass. As she moved the floor ebbed around her feet like the thick current of a lava lamp. It reacted to her steps, fanning out as she stamped, rippling as she slid.

She leaped with both feet. A soft spray of green frothed up when she landed, creamy and slow-motion. She laughed, exhilaration racing through her veins. This was dancing as it should be. Fun and free, with no worries about what she looked like or whether someone would ask her to dance. Or whether she really wanted to dance with that person.

Dancing without fear. Safe, safe dancing.

She danced for what felt like an endless time. She

danced straight lines, she danced circles. When her ankle began throbbing a little, and she'd drunk her fill of the music at last, she adjusted her robe and left the music wing. A smile lingered on her face all the way back to her room. Amazing. How could something as sci-fi or high-tech as that music wing exist here in Permandy? She didn't know how, but she loved it.

She lit her lantern and settled upon the feather-filled padding of her cot to read her adventure novel. Soon her mind raced away to a world of daring treks, rescues, and escapes, all performed by a brave and admirable girl named Danielle.

Hours later the rumbling of Mari's stomach brought her back to reality, jerking her from the middle of Danielle's journey to retrieve a lost amulet. She snapped the book closed, blew out her lantern, and scurried out the door to the food area. By the time she'd gathered her food and sat down to take a bite, her spicy sausage and soft, buttered roll hit her tastebuds like an accusing slap. For Pete's sake, what had she been doing all afternoon? Chatting with Lynia, dancing to wonderfully unearthly music, and reading a novel--while her friends wallowed in dungeons, workhouses, and mines. The Danielle of her novel would never have done that.

She was a terrible, terrible person. She had used her ankle as a pitiful excuse to be selfish and spineless and wimpy. Well, no more.

She finished eating and drained the last of her berry juice with focused determination. Whether she was scared spitless or not, she needed to see if she could help the others.

Right now, she would leave the Haven to trek into Permandy.

Chapter 6

Mari hurried down the rutted road away from the Haven. The gatekeeper had let her out with a detached expression, reminding her that she would need to recite her identification number upon her return. She chanted it under her breath so she wouldn't forget it, the food in her stomach sloshing like an unsettled sea. Her body felt alien, numb, as though she were detached and watching herself scurry along the road like a monastery fugitive.

The coarse robe made her skin itch, but she hadn't dared to wear her normal clothing in Permandy, even under her robe. On the way to the Haven she'd seen other robed figures in the marketplace, so she shouldn't be too conspicuous dressed as she was. She'd left her watch, ring, and earrings in her room, since they looked too modern--even though her earrings were small silver hoops and not the obviously real-world, flashy type like Stefanie wore.

She flipped her hood up and peered at the sun, lowering in the sky. She should have about three hours before the ten o'clock curfew. That should be plenty of time to scout out Randall and Tony's situation so she could come up with a plan. If she could get them free, they could help her figure out how to rescue the others.

When she reached the golden road, she looked in the direction that led away from Permandy. If she didn't have a rescue mission on her agenda, she could escape to another town and flee the Haven for good. She didn't know what made the Magistrate so sure she'd still be at the Haven in three days when the workhouse came to fetch her. Had he not cared, as long as the peasants had been satisfied? But she supposed even if she escaped, she'd either be flagged as a newcomer in the next town, re-captured by soldiers from Permandy, or possibly seized by Shifters.

Not good outcomes, all around. No wonder the Magistrate hadn't been concerned.

She grew closer to the stench and grating bustle of the mines, passing a few cottages and a blacksmith's shop. A wagon piled with hay rumbled by. She darted out of the way of an old man hauling a cart of potatoes, and hurried across the dirt a short distance to the mine barracks. Cringing, she watched soot-covered men and boys hauling rocks from the hillside opening, emerging like weary black ants from an underground anthill. Their faces and arms glistened with sweat, while their ragged clothing was drenched with it. Mari sidled next to the barracks and tried to stay out of sight while she scanned the area for Randall or Tony.

A hissing, slashing noise ending in a sharp crack made her flinch. She looked to see a muscular foreman coiling his arm back, a long whip in his hand. The foreman cursed at a light-haired boy about thirteen who cried out from the lashing.

"You there, speed up!" the foreman bellowed. "The Pit is hungry. We have eight more carts to deliver before nightfall."

Mari pressed her mouth into a taut, worried line. She hoped Randall and Tony hadn't gotten whipped like this boy. And what did the foreman mean that the Pit was hungry--did the Pit *eat* these coal-like rocks? Bizarre. Now she'd heard everything. It reminded her of a frightening dream she'd had once where a deep hole in the ground had tried to swallow a whole city. The only way to stop it was for the city people to shovel coal into it every day.

Spooky, how similar the Pit sounded to that.

The light-haired boy limped away, and she frowned

as she watched him. The boy was teamed with another boy and a man, each connected by shackles on one ankle and a short length of chain. Great. Chains, and the workers were shackled in groups of three. How would she be able to rescue Randall and Tony if they were locked in shackles?

Farther away, another group of three workers appeared at the mouth of the outcropping, carrying rocks. The first worker of the group had distinctively different brown hair, cropped shorter on the sides and a little spiky on top. He bent to dump his armload into the cart. Half a dozen welts crisscrossed his back, his shirt shredded. His face was streaked with dust and sweat.

Randall.

She bit her lip to keep from calling out. The two teen boys shackled with Randall took turns, heaving more rocks into the cart. The cart wobbled as a fine black powder rose up. Someone coughed, and a few yards away, another man groaned. Seeing the foreman stride away down the line barking orders, Mari hurried around the back of the barracks, trying to keep her hood up and the long skirts of her robe out of her way.

"Psst, Randall!" she hissed, when she'd reached the end of the barracks nearest the hillside opening.

Randall spun. Surprise flashed across his face as Mari widened her hood opening to reveal her face. He threw a cautious glance toward the foreman's receding back, then edged closer.

"Mari, what are you doing here? How did you escape?"

"I can come and go for three days," Mari whispered. "Where's Tony? How can I get your shackles off?"

"Tony's delivering carts to the Pit. The shackle keys are on a rope around the foreman's waist.

"Can I get the keys somehow when the foreman

sleeps tonight?"

"No way," Randall said. "Too dangerous. And impossible, since I heard there's a curfew."

The two boys shackled with Randall had paused to listen. "Foreman's about to come back," the taller one said, "but last month I heard him tell a Pit guard that the Magistrate has a master key. It hangs in his building behind his desk, like some fool trophy."

"Okay," Mari said, swallowing a thick lump of dread. "I could try to swipe that when he's out somewhere else."

Randall shook his head. "No, that's suicidal--"

"Back to work," the shorter worker warned, shooting a nervous glance across the mining yard.

Mari ducked behind the barracks while Randall and his crewmates disappeared into the hillside opening. She jogged behind the barracks the way she'd come, and peered around the corner when she reached the roadside edge. The foreman strutted past and clouted a bearded man on the side of the head for no apparent reason. The injustice of the act, mingled with the reek of profuse sweat and greasy rock dust, nearly made her gag.

A hard shell of anger tightened around Mari's fear, quickening her steps to the main road. She pulled her hood almost completely closed, glad for the cover, because she was certain the crazy thing she was about to do was written in bold letters across her face. She dodged a wagon pulled by oxen, and headed toward the center of town. After a few minutes she spotted a young boy tugging a goat along the road by a frayed rope.

"Hello," she said to the boy. "Do you know where the Magistrate's building is?"

The boy nodded. "I'th by the workhou'th," he lisped. "Turn left at the candlemaker'th table."

"Thank you." Mari hurried onward. She reached the marketplace, which looked to be winding down for the day. Chickens squawked, goats bleated. Children quarreled and flitted around the tables. Wiry women scolded the children while they loaded vegetables and woolens into baskets. Next to a man selling red beans and new potatoes, Mari spotted the candlemaker's table, displaying wooden boxes of beeswax candles. The candlemaker was also packing up. Mari looked left. Yes, that's the direction the soldiers had taken Stefanie, and the lisping boy had said the Magistrate's building was near the workhouse.

She angled off the golden road and walked a dirt street until she saw a wide stone building with two soldiers standing outside, flanking the door. Peering around the edges of her hood, she circled the building, scoping it out. No back door. Two windows without glass, one on the side and one in the back, with the shutters half open. Through the windows she heard the Magistrate's reedy voice droning in a bitter tirade against restless and demanding peasants, the annoyances of tending the Pit, and the hassles of dealing with Shifters. She glimpsed an armored shoulder of a soldier inside.

Great. Guarded inside and out. Not very convenient. What should she do now? Without the key, she wouldn't be able to free Randall and Tony. Tears prickling her eyes, she drifted away. So much for all the bravery she'd mustered. She wouldn't have an opportunity to use it.

Although she could visit the workhouse and check out Stefanie's situation, since she was close. Yes, that's what she would do. She continued along the street until she came to a long wooden building with "Workhouse" carved above the doorway. A woman with a lined, hard face stood sweeping the steps.

"Excuse me, ma'am," Mari said, being careful not to lift her head too far. "Have you seen that blonde newcomer who was brought here this morning?"

The woman shrugged. "Yeah. Grouchy young thing. Shortage of servant help around these parts lately, so she was placed right away. Good riddance. She's working at a farm south of here."

Mari murmured a dejected thanks and trudged away. Dang. She'd gotten here too late to intervene for Stefanie. How would they ever all get back together?

She approached the Magistrate's building again and gave it a frustrated glance. Still guarded of course. No sense hanging out here. She'd have better luck trying to steal the keys off the foreman while he slept than trying to get in this guarded building. But there was the issue of the curfew that messed up that idea. She'd have to go back to the Haven tonight and ponder the situation.

As she reached the Magistrate's building, a motion on the road in front of her snagged her attention. A lean figure came racing up the road, panting, his shirt flapping with the frenzy of his run. He stumbled, kicking up a flurry of dust, and caught himself. The guards tensed as he hurtled toward the front door of the Magistrate's building.

"Shifters are comin'!" the man shouted. "I saw 'em on the hillside headin' this way. Warn the Magistrate!"

Inside, the Magistrate gave a bellow of surprise, apparently having heard through the window. Right then, the distant rhythm of pounding horses' hooves began to shake the air.

The Magistrate burst from the building in full rant, followed by three soldiers. "They're not going to bully and push me around this time, I tell you. I don't have to answer to them. I'll be danged if I'll turn all five newcomers over to these fanatic fools. It's my village, and I make the decisions around here."

A jolt of fear surged through Mari. Shifters, here? She retreated to hide behind the Magistrate's building, her heart slamming in her chest. At the same time, she saw through the half-open back window that the Magistrate's one-room building now stood empty. No guards. No one. She swallowed.

Insanity. Her only chance to get the key, right as dangerous Shifters arrived.

Hooves thundered up the street, and horses snorted and whinnied. She peeked around the corner of the building to see five riders reign in their mounts in front of the Magistrate, their black cloaks billowing in the whirling dust. Triangles of gold gleamed at their throats, serving as clasps to their cloaks. Scattered townspeople stood close by, looking fearful but curious.

"You--Magistrate. Where are the newcomers that arrived earlier today?" a chillingly familiar, harsh voice demanded. "And don't try to tell us they didn't arrive. We know the Portal's been open since sunset last night, and an old man's sister in Golmer told us there were five young strangers on the way to your village."

"They've already been placed, Bierce," the Magistrate responded, though sounding less blustery than a minute ago. "They were mine to deal with."

Mari's adrenalin kicked in as Bierce answered the Magistrate. Her mind reeled from the comment about a Portal, but she had to move fast if she was going to steal the key. No one loitered behind the building to sound an alarm, since the people that had been milling about had moved to watch the Magistrate's' encounter with the Shifters. She edged around the opened shutter and hoisted herself into the window, struggling against the length of her robe for a moment before swinging into the room. Dropping to her feet with a bit of a thud, she froze. The front door was ajar.

"I sent the two boys to the mines," the Magistrate was saying in begrudging voice. "Near the Pit. The three girls I sold, to work overseas. They went by wagon early this morning to the port of Ranser."

Bierce's cursing response and grating growl of frustration came through the door and windows. Mari's eyes slid to the wall behind a wooden desk. A long metal key hung there on a nail. In three quick steps, she whipped over and snatched the key off the nail. She dashed back to the window, heaved herself up, and clambered back outside. Her legs trembled as she paused at the corner of the building, the key clutched in her hand. Breathing through her mouth, she tried to muster enough courage to slip across the street in plain view. She had to try to make it to the mines before the Shifters did.

"Very well," Bierce's steely voice said. "We'll round up the two boys now and spend the night at the Permandy Inn. In the morning we'll set off for the seacoast to fetch the girls. Perhaps the boat hasn't sailed yet. For your sake, Magistrate, I hope it hasn't."

"I should be able to place strangers as I see fit," the Magistrate grumbled.

"You have clear orders to detain newcomers," Bierce snapped. "I don't appreciate your lack of compliance. This is your warning, sir. Heed it, or the future consequences will be severe."

Mari adjusted her hood and glided across the street, reaching the cover of another building as the Magistrate muttered a response she couldn't hear.

"Right now we need some water," Bierce ordered. "Quickly. For the horses as well as my men."

In the midst of the Magistrate's instructions to the

harsh Shifter about the location of a horse trough and a rainwater barrel, Mari fled. She sprinted as though a pack of demons pursued her, back to the golden road and on toward the mines. The sight of townspeople, animals, and wagons passed in a frenzied blur. Slowing as she neared the mines, she scanned the plodding mine workers, noting the location of the foreman with his whip to her left. She spotted Tony as he toiled by the front end of the barracks. Black dust covered his face and clothing, and sweat soaked his lacerated shirt.

The edges of the key pressed into her palm as she clutched it. Tears stung her eyes. Like Randall, Tony had gotten whipped, while she'd been leisurely eating meat rolls, reading, and dancing. She hurried to hide by the barracks. When the foreman stomped away to berate a distant worker, Mari leaned out to catch Tony's eye.

"Tony!" she called.

Tony lifted his head in confusion, and looked around.

"Over here by the barracks," Mari said. "It's me, Mari."

"Mari," Tony said, breaking into a wide grin as he saw her robed form. "Sweet! Have you come to rescue me?"

"I have a master key for your shackle--" Mari began, then broke off as she saw the foreman pivoting to return. She slipped behind the barracks again, her heart pounding, ticking off the seconds. Blast. How would she be able to release both Tony and Randall at this rate? Soon the Shifters and their horses would be finishing in town, and in a few short minutes they'd be here.

The foreman barked orders for Tony's group to haul their cart to a clearing fifty feet away. Mari gnawed her lip. Dang. Okay, she'd have to release Randall first, then come back for Tony. She ran behind the barracks to the far end by the mine opening, and saw that Randall and his group had just finished dumping their armloads of rock into a cart. The foreman was turned away. Good timing. She darted to Randall and crouched at his feet, her fingers shaking as she jammed the key into the shackle and wiggled it. The shackle sprang open.

"You got the key," Randall said in stunned disbelief.

"Yes," Mari said, "but Shifters will be here in a couple of minutes. We have to scoot, and I mean fast." Crouched below the cart line, she also unlocked the shackles of the other two workers. She kicked the chain and shackles under the cart, and dashed with Randall and the other two boys to hide behind the barracks.

The taller boy nodded at a growth of trees and shrubs ten yards away, beyond the mine opening. "We can make a run for those trees, then cut south across the fields to Lisden. My aunt lives there and will let us stay. I'm only wanted here as slave labor because my parents died a few months ago. Permandy shackles orphans for Pit work."

"What about Tony?" Mari whispered in a panic.

"No time," the shorter boy said, his expression grim. "I hear horses."

Mari tensed, hearing the low shuddering of horses' hooves. The sound increased in volume.

Randall shot a look across the mining yard and grabbed Mari's wrist. "Everyone's watching the road. Let's go!"

The four of them ran helter-skelter for the trees. When they got there, they ducked down, their breathing ragged. Mari looked through the bushes. The Shifters appeared, galloping from the glittery golden road onto the dirt area bordering the mines. A stocky rider with graying hair raised an imperious arm to hail the foreman, then spoke. Mari couldn't hear the words, but the Shifter's voice sounded harsh and steely.

Bierce, no question about it.

Mari watched Bierce trade a terse conversation with the foreman. The foreman gestured toward the mine entrance and then pointed at Tony, who stood twenty yards away, staring at the riders. Bierce dismounted and strode over to Tony. The other Shifters followed, their postures looking almost hungry, predatory. Bierce seized Tony's arm and yanked up Tony's shirt sleeve. The triumphant noise of Bierce's reaction made Mari shudder.

"Tony belongs to the Shifters now," the taller boy said, rising into a careful stand. "Let's hoof it before they notice we're gone."

"Wait, Kale," Randall said. "Mari and I have to find the other girls, Stef and Lauren."

"The Shifters will get to them before we do," Kale said.

"Maybe not," Mari said, tying the loose end of her robe belt around the key for safekeeping. "The Magistrate told the Shifters about Randall and Tony, but he said he sold us girls to work somewhere overseas. The Shifters are going to a place called Ranser tomorrow, to try to intercept the boat."

"That'll keep them busy for a couple of days," the shorter boy said. "Ranser's quite a trip, even on horseback."

Kale nodded his agreement. "If the Shifters are heading for Ranser in the morning, you two can come back tomorrow for your gal friends."

"All right," Randall said. "Let's go."

68

They ran, keeping low behind the cover of the trees and bushes, moving deeper into the fields and countryside. The discordant sounds and rank smells of the mines faded. After about fifteen minutes, however, Mari's ankle began a fierce throbbing, and she slowed, limping.

Randall frowned and slowed with her. "Your spider bite?"

"Yeah." Mari winced.

"Vampire spider?" Kale asked with concern, circling back to walk next to her.

Mari nodded.

"You need ointment on that," Kale said. "And you shouldn't be running so much on it."

"We don't have much of a choice," Randall said.

The shorter boy eyed Mari's ankle, then the setting sun. "She's gonna slow us down. We'll never make it to Lisden by curfew."

Mari groaned. "That stupid curfew. How far away is Lisden?"

"Another four, maybe five miles," Kale said. "We'll have to keep a fast pace to reach it by sunset."

"I could go back to the Haven," Mari said reluctantly. "It's closer and the ointment's there. Food too. The Shifters will be busy for another two days, so I should be safe."

"Okay, I'll meet you back in Permandy tomorrow," Randall said. "We'll hunt for Stef and Lauren in the morning. Bring that key in case it also opens Lauren's cell."

Mari nodded. "But Stefanie's not at the workhouse. She got sent south to some farm."

Randall swore, and shook his head.

"And you can't be seen in Permandy," Mari said. "It's too obvious you're a newcomer--and a mine

69

escapee, with that torn shirt."

The shorter boy spat in the grass. "Yeah. Don't risk it."

"Fine," Randall said with irritation. "Mari, meet me behind the treeline at noon, but not too close to the mines. Be careful. If you're able to free Lauren, bring her and we can take her back to Lisden. If not, we can plan more tomorrow."

"Okay," Mari said.

"We need to go," Kale said, his eyes restless and his legs twitchy with nerves. "Unless we want to stay here in the fields tonight where there isn't an enforced curfew." He started off through the grass. "Me, I always feel safer in a cottage."

The shorter boy followed and, after a short hesitation, so did Randall.

Mari began limping back toward Permandy, her mind whirling. Mental images of whips and mining carts mingled with snorting horses and gold triangles glinting on Shifters' cloaks. What an exhausting, confusing day. She sure hoped Tony would be all right until they could figure out a way to rescue him from the Shifters.

And blast this curfew thing. She'd better make it back to the Haven in time. It sounded like the curfew was only enforced near the villages. She was tempted to try to sleep in the field tonight, since they'd been safe enough by Pod's burned cottage last night, but Kale's reservations spooked her.

She should've asked Kale what the penalty for breaking the curfew was.

Hobbling along at a fair pace despite the pain pulsing in her ankle, Mari reached the outskirts of Permandy as the sun reached the distant hills and sank like a glowing stone behind them. The countryside seemed eerily quiet, with no sign of townspeople. Only a few windows radiated a faint yellow light. Sheep and goats and chickens huddled together in the grass and on the dirt, not making a sound.

Mari's feet crunched onto the main road. The golden color of the road appeared sickly and greenish with the black-light effect from the moon. Shadows cloaked trees, goat pens, and piles of hay.

Ten o'clock, and darkness. The sun had set. She hadn't made it back before curfew.

She quickened her pace, watching the shadows with growing dread. Were any of them moving? Motionless tree shadows...motionless cottage shadows...all motionless so far. Good. Her breathing rasped in the silent moonlight, shallow and quick. Fifty feet ahead, she glimpsed the tree-lined dirt road that led to the Haven. Safety lay within reach.

A scant second later, a shadow moved over by the blacksmith's shop. Mari saw a tall and bulky shadow detach from the darkness and began to move toward her. Swiftly it moved, towering over seven feet tall. Black booted feet, muscular legs. Powerful shoulders and arms, bare and flexing in the moonlight. A wrestler's shape, a man--yet an inhuman, demented man.

Shivers rippled down Mari's arms and spine in repeated waves, and she clenched her teeth together. Her legs turned to water. This silent figure possessed a black-hooded face, exactly like the one in her nightmare at twelve years old. He had blank slits for eyes, and wielded a huge glinting axe over one broad shoulder.

It was the Executioner. She'd broken curfew, and he was coming for her.

Chapter 7

Mari's terror turned to pure, panicked adrenalin, pumping speed into her weary muscles. She careened onto the rutted dirt road leading to the Haven, heedless of her ankle pain. Her hood whipped back from her head as she ran. She looked back and confirmed what she already knew. The Executioner followed her, his legs taking long strides, his double half-mooned axe gleaming like a madman's in the moonlight.

She stumbled on her robe and continued to run, raw and crazy with horror. Her lungs burned. Her legs and her ankle ached. The shadowed trees lining the road blurred by. She hitched her robe skirts up away from her shins, so she could run faster. It worked until the robe folds caught and bunched between her knees, throwing her legs off rhythm. With a tooth-wrenching jolt, she fell, tumbling across the dirt of the road. She skidded across the ruts. Her vision spun as she rolled to a standstill, stunned, sprawled on the ground like a chicken ready for beheading.

Her strength wilted as death strode toward her. The Executioner's powerful arms gathered force for the strike. His stride lengthened. His blade raised from his shoulder, swinging in a hissing arc through the night air.

The axe plunged downward. Mari yelped and rolled. The axe blade thudded mere inches from where her head had been, spraying dirt and rocks. She writhed off the road and staggered to her feet, aiming for the nearest tree. *Quick.* She needed cover, protection. The Executioner shouldered his axe again and followed, the vacant slits of his eyes showing no mercy. On rubbery legs, she dodged behind a tree. The axe splintered wood and bark behind her with a crashing impact. Mari spun toward the road again, her heart sledgehammering against her ribs.

No, not the trees. The gate. She had to reach the safety of the Haven gate. The iron bars now stood visible in the gloomy darkness, waiting fifty feet away in impassive silence. The Executioner's footsteps thumped behind her. How far behind, she didn't know, or want to turn to see.

"Open the gate!" she screamed, seeing the silhouette of the gatekeeper through the shelter window by the fence. "Let me in!"

The gatekeeper shot to his feet and scurried out of the shelter. "I need your number," he called in a shaky voice, eyeing the monstrosity pursuing her. "No one re-enters the Haven without a number."

"I--I can't remember," Mari yelled. "Just let me inside."

The gatekeeper shook his head, but he fumbled with his keys, getting them ready. "I need a number, miss. It's the rules."

Mari reached the gate and slammed into it, her fists clenching the bars. She swore. "113911--no, that's not it. 319119?" Her voice came out hoarse, broken. She threw a glance behind her, where the Executioner advanced, now thirty feet away. "133199? Or wait--131199! *That's it. Open the freaking gate!*"

The gatekeeper nodded and jammed the key into the lock. It clicked open.

Mari looked back. The Executioner strode toward her, twenty feet away.

The gate swung open.

Fifteen feet. The axe lifted from the Executioner's shoulder. His black boots took long steps. Ten feet, eight--

Mari lunged, falling inside the gate, and the

gatekeeper slammed it closed. The lock clicked a split second before the axe came down against the bars and sent a tremendous scraping clang into the night air.

The gatekeeper fell backward, sitting hard on the ground.

Twisting onto her back, Mari threw a horrified glance upward at the Executioner's massive bulk standing at the gate. The dark beheader's slotted eyes regarded her malevolently for a tense, silent moment before he spun and stalked back down the dirt road, away from the Haven.

"Well, miss," the gatekeeper exclaimed. "I think you need to be more heedful of the curfew hour from now on."

Various retorts sprang into Mari's mind, none of them polite. She dragged herself into a shaky stand and gave the gatekeeper a withering look. She trudged across the courtyard, into the Haven, and straight to the nursing wing. The white-robed nurse caught sight of her and frowned.

"What have you been doing, young lady?" the nurse exclaimed. "You're filthy. And you're late for your evening ointment."

"Yes, I know," Mari said, sinking onto a stool. She stuck her foot out for the ointment application.

The nurse pursed her lips. "Looks swollen. You've been walking on that ankle too much." She jabbed a stiff finger toward an archway to their left. "First, bathe in the hot-spring while I fetch you a clean robe."

Mari sighed and obeyed. She endured the indignity of a chamber pot, removed her dirt-scuffed robe, and slipped into the hot, steaming water of the hot-spring room. Her eyes closed as her head leaned against the smooth stone sides. Wow. She'd used up a lifetime's worth of adrenalin tonight. How could it be, that the

Being from her blackest childhood nightmare enforced the curfew here in Permandy? She couldn't take any more of this dimension. She would die here, and Randall and the others too.

Her mother must be worried sick, totally frantic by now. Stefanie's father would've told her mother that she and Randall had disappeared from the party, vanished without a trace for the last twenty-four hours. Uncle Jim and Aunt Lacey would be worried too.

The nurse's voice interrupted her depressing thoughts. "Here's a clean robe and a drying towel. Throw your dirty robe in the community laundry bin when you return to the living quarters."

"Okay." Mari listened to the nurse's footsteps recede, then washed her hair, finished bathing, and dressed. She shook out the dirty robe and held it up. Hey. If she was able to release Lauren tomorrow, she could use this extra robe to smuggle Lauren out of Permandy.

A definite stroke of good luck, this extra robe.

She suffered through the nurse's further chidings and the ointment application, and walked to her room. Her ankle ached. The filtered moonglow from her skylight illuminated the adventure novel which lay on the bed with her jeans and normal top. She shook her head, tossing the old robe with the key on the floor. What a joke. She didn't need to read adventure novels in this dimension--here, she lived them. Harrowing escapes and daring rescues were definitely overrated. She'd much rather read about them. Like romance, adventures were a lot more stressful in real life; in fact, they pretty much sucked. Right now, she felt so drained, all she wanted to do was throw herself on her bed and bawl like a third grader.

Ugh. Her father would be thoroughly ashamed of

her for that kind of outburst.

With weary arms, she shoved her book and clothes off the bed. Her hair was still damp, but she curled up under the blanket, not bothering to remove her Haven shoes. Her eyes closed like leaden shades. At least tonight Randall would be safe in Lisden with Kale. She'd worry about finding the others tomorrow....

She awoke in the semi-darkness with a sharp intake of breath. Her heart beat a little too fast. Though she couldn't remember exactly what she'd been dreaming about, it hadn't been good. Something murky about scuttling hairy spiders and shadows with gaping mouths. Ugh. She stretched, turning onto her back. She didn't know what time it was, but it felt like she'd only been asleep a few hours. She glanced at her skylight. Still dark. She'd try to go back to sleep.

As she closed her eyes again, an image of Tony and his enthusiastic grin popped into her mind. How sad-- he'd been so happy to see her at the mines, thinking she'd been about to rescue him. But she'd failed to free him. What was happening to him, in the clutches of the Shifters? And what had that Bierce guy said to the Magistrate about a *Portal?* Did he mean a gateway into this dimension--and was that how she and the others had traveled here?

That's what it sounded like.

Other unsettling thoughts sprang up and raced around her brain like ugly zombies on caffeine. In this mess of a dimension, the triangles meant something. Not only were triangles branded upon their forearms, but the Shifters used them for cloak clasps. A triangle had been etched onto the cave wall somehow. Was the cave triangle the Portal, or did it mark the Portal?

She sighed. Who knew. She hoped Lauren was getting fed in Isolation. Perhaps she should bring

Lauren some food tomorrow, especially if the master key didn't fit the cell lock and she had to leave Lauren there. And Stefanie? She imagined Stefanie kneeling like Cinderella in a decrepit cottage somewhere, with her snug designer jeans ragged and torn, scrubbing floors with broken fingernails, her mascara blurred and raccoon-like around her weeping eyes.

Mari twitched. Her eyes snapped open. Her woolen blanket began to feel itchy, her legs restless. With an annoyed growl, she sat up. She couldn't go back to sleep with all these weighty issues stomping through her consciousness. Maybe the Calming Room in the music wing would help soothe her.

Hopefully the Haven didn't shut that wing down at night.

She slipped into the hall and padded toward the music room. No one wandered the halls except one hooded soul, who turned off at the library wing and disappeared inside. She reached the music wing. In the entryway, as before, faint strains of blended sound swirled from the three rooms. She stepped closer to the Invigorating room and caught an earful of a jazzy, lively beat. Interesting. But that wasn't what she wanted right now. She headed left and opened the Calming Room door.

Inside, the entire room flowed with shades of blue. A feathery, light blue made up the walls and ceiling, and a medium, serene blue colored the woolens draped over benches along the room's edges. The floor featured the darkest blue, calm and velvety in appearance. The floor reacted to her feet as the Joyous Room's floor had, except much slower.

Even the music sounded blue. Soft-sweet instruments, perhaps violins and flutes, played in a hushed stream of drawn-out notes. The sounds drifted in from an unknown source, and Mari's breathing slowed to match its rhythm. She swayed and closed her eyes. Yes. This is what she needed.

After a few minutes she opened her eyes, feeling more relaxed already. Only one other person occupied the room, a tall man about twenty, lean and olive-skinned. He swayed across the room about thirty feet away. He glanced her way, gave a distant nod, and continued his dancing.

Mari fell back into her own dancing. She dipped and turned, meandered and sashayed. Her arms lifted high. She spiraled like a gentle seedpod in the air. The music entwined with her body, and her body floated as if it were in a light breeze on a summer's day. Her robe skirts swished. She felt peaceful, and at this point in time, nothing mattered except the music. A smile spread across her face, and her eyes closed again.

In a few seconds, her eyes eased back open. Startled, she found the lean man dancing a mere five feet from her, watching her with curiosity. Up close he looked Greek or Middle Eastern, with large dark eyes and a slender nose. Exotic. A small gold loop hung from his left ear.

She turned away, unsure whether to be flattered or annoyed. Why was he studying her with that amused look on his face--did she look lame when she danced this way? Was her hair sticking up from going to sleep on it damp? She huffed, and watched the man out the corners of her eyes. He faced the blue sky of the wall again, not paying attention to her any longer. His body moved in smooth arcs. Muscular, with a powerful, catlike kind of grace that reminded her of a sleek panther.

Giving herself a mental shake, she ran her fingers through her hair and relaxed back into the music's beat.

She danced until her gaze focused on the robed figure again. At the same time, the man's head turned. Their eyes locked, riveted into place. One black eyebrow tilted upward a fraction. She slowed as the man glided toward her. With his expression darkly sober, he stretched his hand toward her and gave a small bow.

She stared at his hand. Was he actually offering to dance with her?

She hesitated. Brad's teasing face flashed across her mind's eye, as well as two other boyfriends, long gone. She shouldn't trust anyone, shouldn't open herself up and be vulnerable again.

Or did it really matter, here?

No, it didn't. To heck with it. She could die in this forsaken dimension tomorrow. It was only one dance. Her hand stretched out, almost of its own accord. She saw it, small and tapered, reaching across the rhythmic space between them. His large hand closed easily over hers, the clasp strong and warm. She thought she saw a flicker of surprise touch his face at the contact, and then it was gone.

They danced together. The awkward corners of their motions melted away after a short while. The music fused them to one purpose as they translated sounds into turns and arm movements and footsteps. They became a unit, flowing together. Long before Mari felt ready to quit, the music began to grow softer, fading from the room.

The man looked upward, as though watching the music seep into the ceiling. His eyes closed briefly. When he opened them, he walked to the door. She trailed after him. New music crept in, a melodious burbling that sounded like a mountain stream.

He focused on her face, his eyes luminous, his expression serious. "Your name?" His deep voice came out smooth, but his question sounded abbreviated, as though words were almost too much after their dancing and the music.

"Mari," she said in a near-whisper.

He gave a slight nod. "Sanjen," he said, introducing himself, and gave a slight bow before he walked from the room.

Early the next morning after catching a few more hours of sleep, Mari headed away from the Haven with her hood flipped up. She clutched a basket she'd found in the eating area. In it she'd stashed the extra robe, two rolls, an apple, and a sausage. She'd tucked the key under the robe she wore, out of sight and kept snug by her bra strap. It was a sheer miracle that the key hadn't worked itself loose from the robe tie during her mad dash to escape the Executioner.

She'd been very, very lucky.

Throwing a glance upward, she saw the sky darkening and collecting clouds. A light sprinkle of rain hit her nose, and she groaned. Great. Sloshing around on primitive dirt roads in the rain. What next?

She reached the golden road and followed it into town. The rain grew heavier, turning the glittery dust into an ochre-colored mess. The marketplace in Permandy appeared desolate and miserable, with a meager showing of villagers huddled under makeshift cloth tents, selling their wares. A few hardy souls dashed from table to table, conducting their business and leaving in a hurry.

Mari huddled over her basket to keep the contents dry. She halted on the side of the road and waited for a wagon to pass, and stared at the back of her hand as a large splash of rain hit it. *Gray.* The rain was turning gray, opaque and slimy, and growing thicker by the second. She shook the ooze off her hand. Disgusting! What was this, some sort of gunky fallout? None of the villagers acted as though it was anything unusual.

It figured. Another warped part of this dimension.

She made her way to the area where the Magistrate had divided her from the others. The path the two soldiers had taken Lauren down lay on the opposite side of the road, past an empty market table. She started to slosh across the road, when she caught sight of a pair of Shifters on horseback tromping up the mucky road toward her. Their black cloaks hung thick with slime, their horses too. They wore their cloak hoods up, which covered their features and gave them a sinister, faceless appearance, like that of Death on horseback.

Mari took a quick step back, her heart beating faster. Dang--hadn't the Shifters left for Ranser yet? She hung her head low so that no part of her face showed. The Shifters rode by, cursing the slime rain in specific and the landscape in general.

"I doubt we'll find that other kid anyway," one of them grumbled. "He's long gone, probably to another village."

The other Shifter grunted a response of agreement.

"Bierce won't know how long we've searched here if he's in Ranser," the first Shifter said, his voice fading with distance. "Like you, I detest the Permandy Inn--and now, this weather. I'm all for taking that Tony kid back to the Fortress today instead of tomorrow. What do you think?"

The other Shifter's response was swallowed up in the soggy bleating of a nearby goat, and the blopping sound of the slime rain.

Mari stood at the road's edge, her muscles tense. It sounded like the Shifters had split up earlier this morning, with Bierce and two others riding to Ranser, and these two staying behind to search for Randall. It also sounded like Tony remained here, perhaps stashed at the Permandy Inn where the Shifters were staying. Was Tony tied up or shackled in their room? She wished she could check out his situation somehow.

She breathed a deep sigh. With Shifters roaming the town, that would be impossible as well as highly risky. Her priority was to find Lauren and see whether or not the master key opened her cell.

Holding her hood around her face, she crossed the road and made her way down a side street, past a long row of huge wooden barrels and stacked crates. A warm blob of rain the consistency of rubber cement dripped from the top of her hood and splattered onto her mouth. She spat. It tasted like rubber cement, too.

"Oh, for Pete's sake!" she hissed.

She shook her hand clean and started to wipe the rest of the goo from her face. But before she could, a strong arm shot out from behind her, wrapping around her waist and dragging her behind a stack of crates.

Chapter 8

Mari struggled, drawing in her breath to scream, tasting slime rain and blinded by her hood. *Did she dare scream and attract attention?* She heard the apple from her basket fall and thump onto the ground.

"Shhh, Mari! Don't scream," the owner of the arm said in a low voice. "It's me--Randall."

The arm around Mari's waist relaxed as she stopped struggling. She twisted to face her mugger. It was Randall all right, wearing a short, slime-covered cloak that looked like a hooded poncho, and a pair of villager trousers and shoes. She smeared the slime from her mouth, her fright morphing into anger. "What do you mean, grabbing me like that?" she whispered heatedly. "You really scared--"

"Don't get all huffy," Randall cut in. "I wanted to pull you over before anyone saw us. There are Shifters running around here."

"No, really?" Mari said. "That's exactly why you shouldn't be here in Permandy. I thought you were going to meet me behind the treeline by the mines."

Randall shrugged. "Kale had these extra clothes, so I came disguised."

A wagon driven by an elderly man creaked by, silencing them for a moment.

"How'd you know it was me, anyway?" Mari asked, after the wagon had passed.

"Not too many monk-robed people say, 'for Pete's sake' like Grandma Stratton."

"Oh." Mari shook her head. Whatever. She huddled further behind the crates, keeping her voice soft. "So, have you found the Isolation place?"

"Yep. It's down this road and off to the left. Long stone building with barred windows. Only one soldier

83

there, and I saw Lauren in the end cell. If we made some sort of distraction on the other end, we might have time to unlock the door."

"Distraction, like what?"

"I dunno. You think of something for once."

"For once?" Mari repeated, glaring at the sullen expression on his face and feeling almost sorry she'd freed him from his shackle.

"Yeah, for once," Randall grumbled. "Instead of running off and hiding in your happy little Haven. I found Stef this morning, so it's your turn to do something."

"You found Stefanie? Why are you so freaking grouchy, then, if you found her?"

Randall's eyebrows gathered into a stormy frown. "Kale's aunt heard that a newcomer girl got placed at a farm a mile or two from their cottage. On the way here this morning I took a detour and stopped by. I saw Stef scrubbing the front porch, but this white-haired maniac of a woman came out and set the watchdogs on me." He flicked a torn spot on his pants leg. "So I had to scram."

"At least we know where she is," Mari said. She picked up the apple from the ground and grimaced. Ugh, bruised and slimed. She tossed it away. "Does Lauren know you're here?"

He shook his head. "I tried to talk to her through the barred window when the guard went around the corner, but I guess she couldn't hear me. I didn't want to call too loudly."

"Hmm." Mari adjusted the extra robe in her basket to cover the roll and sausage. Seeing Randall's questioning eyebrows, she explained. "Food and another monk's robe, for Lauren."

He gave a reluctant nod. "Good idea."

A prickly sense of irritation rose in Mari as she

84

leaned out to check the road. Like their father, Randall had a definite problem admitting she'd done something well. "Show me where she is," she said.

Randall led her down the street and turned left. There sat an ugly stone building, made uglier by the slime on it. A grizzled-looking soldier strolled the windowed side that faced them. They took a side street and hid behind a hay wagon.

"Lauren's on that closer end," Randall said. "If you could go ask the guard a question, like maybe directions to somewhere, I could unlock the cell. Except he might recognize you."

"He'd recognize both of us," Mari said. "He was with the Magistrate yesterday morning. Too bad Kale didn't come with you."

"Kale's a mine escapee. They stick orphans on mine duty in Permandy. He's safe in Lisden, so he stayed there."

"Oh." Mari glanced down at her basket again, and an idea began to form in her head. It wasn't the greatest idea, but it had potential. "How about if we nab some little kid walking by and ask him to give this food to the guard?" she said. "I hate to use the food I brought for Lauren, but one of us could unlock the cell while the guard is occupied."

Randall looked doubtful. "Why would a little kid want to do that, instead of just running off with the food?"

"Um, because I'll find a girl and let her keep the basket for a payment?"

"Right," Randall scoffed. "She could run off with both, if she wanted."

Mari glared. "Maybe she won't think of that."

"You're way too trusting."

"*You're* way too negative."

85

"It'd be a waste of Lauren's food. You don't think things through. We don't even know if this is the right key."

True. Mari swallowed a growing lump of nervousness. "We won't know until we try," she said. "We have to try something--" She broke off, seeing two girls about eight or nine years old slogging up the side street through the gray slime. One of them lugged a butter churn. Seeing the guard turn his back to stroll away from them, Mari dashed over with her basket. Behind her, Randall made an irritated noise.

"Hello," Mari said to the girls, trying not to show too much of her face. "That churn sure looks heavy."

"It is!" the skinnier one piped up. "We're taking turns carrying it home. Mama had the wood man fix it."

Mari threw a glance back at Randall, who was glaring at her. "Would you two do me a big favor?" she asked the girls. "I have this food for the Isolation cell guard, but my ankle is bothering me. Could you give it to him? I'll let you keep this nice basket as a thank you."

The butter churn girl's eyes grew round, and she set the churn down. "Yes! Mama would love a basket like that."

The skinnier girl bounced up and down. "It's a good basket," she chirped.

Mari removed the extra robe, and handed the basket and food over. "Thanks. Don't tell him it's from me, just say you're giving it to him because he looks hungry. I'll watch your churn while you do that." She took the churn and stepped quickly back to Randall as the girls set off. The girls giggled, holding their hands over the sausage and rolls like small umbrellas against the falling slime.

Mari snatched the key from inside her robe, and

handed it to Randall along with the extra robe. "Go!" she urged.

Randall let out a forceful exhale and left the cover of the wagon, hurrying toward the Isolation building. In a flash, he disappeared around the corner of it.

Holding her breath, Mari watched the girls. The guard observed the giggling pair with boredom as they approached, but his bushy eyebrows raised as they trotted closer and slowed in shyness. Mari heard their high-pitched chatter over the sounds of the dropping slime. The skinnier girl tipped the basket to show the food, eliciting a lopsided grin from the guard.

"Come on, Randall," Mari muttered, darting a glance at the other end of the building. No sign of either Randall or Lauren yet. Had the key fit?

The guard took the food. He bit into the sausage like a ravenous animal while the girls waved farewell and sludged back across the road with the basket.

Mari forced a smile as the girls reached the wagon. "Thanks a lot, girls. Good job. Enjoy the basket."

"We will," the skinnier girl said. They collected the butter churn and went on their way.

A tense minute or two passed. Mari scanned the Isolation building as well as the streets. Where were Randall and Lauren? Had a villager spotted Lauren escaping? It seemed unlikely. Mari hadn't heard a commotion or a cry for the guard. Maybe Randall and Lauren were hiding somewhere for a while. She hoped the two Shifters hadn't materialized nearby.

The guard finished with the sausage and rolls. He gave an open-mouthed belch and ambled to the other side of the building, out of sight. Mari chewed her lip. She hoped Randall hadn't left the cell door wide open, or the guard would immediately start searching. Leaning away from the wagon, she listened for any sort of telltale sound. She heard nothing.

"Psst!"

Mari swiveled to look behind her, where the sound had come from. Randall stood in his slime-smeared poncho at the other end of the street, impatiently waving her over. A tall, monk-hooded figure stood next to him. Lauren. Trembling with relief, Mari hurried over.

"What took so long?" she asked Randall as they started walking.

"Didn't want to come back around near the guard, and then we hid so Lauren could put on the robe."

"Are you okay?" Mari asked Lauren, facing her so she could lip-read.

Lauren nodded. "Starved though. They gave me a piece of stale bread yesterday that I didn't eat. Today, I got so hungry it started to look good."

Mari wrinkled her nose and began to comment when Randall grabbed her upper arm. "Hey, talk later. Let's get to Lisden so we can get out of this snot rain."

"You're really gross, you know that?" Mari growled. Ugh, snot rain, like snot dripping from the sky. Not an image she wished to dwell on.

Randall walked faster and didn't respond.

They slogged through mucky puddles on the formerly golden road, making their way through Permandy's light traffic of wagons and townspeople. Mari clenched her hands into fists, darting jittery looks around the marketplace, expecting Shifters on horseback to ride past at any minute. Or almost as bad, to see the Magistrate patrolling with his guards as he searched for his missing master key.

On the other end of town, Randall threw a wary glance at the mining yard as they passed it. The workers loaded the carts, the slick gray of the weather splattered onto their blackened clothing and faces. A minute later, Mari shuddered as she passed the blacksmith's shop. She half-feared a looming black shape with an axe would detach from the sides of the shop and stride after her. She saw the road to the Haven a short distance ahead of them. A glimmer of safety lay there. But was the plan for her to abandon the Haven for good at this point, and head to Lisden? Her stomach fluttered with nerves. They had to decide what to do, now that they'd freed Lauren.

"Well," she said, keeping her voice low, "Good thing that key worked."

Randall snorted. "That was one moronic guard. That food could've been poisoned for all he knew. It was sheer luck that your flimsy idea worked."

"You asked me to come up with an idea, so I did," Mari said.

"Yeah," Randall said, "and now Lauren doesn't have any food." He turned to Lauren. "Do you have enough energy to walk five miles?"

"I'm sorry, what?" Lauren said, embarrassment coloring her face. When Randall repeated the question louder, Lauren nodded. "I think so. I feel weak and shaky, but I'll manage."

"Oh, I didn't tell you guys," Mari said, "the Shifters I saw said something about Tony. I think he's still here in Permandy, maybe at the Inn. We could try to rescue him."

"No," Randall said. "I'm taking Lauren to safety first. Sneaking Tony out under a couple of Shifters' noses doesn't sound appealing. Rescuing Stefanie is more possible than that."

They'd almost reached the road to the Haven. Mari slowed. "Well, I'm going back to the Haven," she announced. "I need more ointment and rest for my ankle, and my real clothes are still in there."

"Are you kidding?" Randall asked, swiveling to glare at her. "We can't be separated now. And we need to figure out a way to rescue Stefanie."

"You don't like my ideas anyway--you go rescue her."

"Stop being a brat, Mari Leigh," Randall said. "You have to come with us."

Mari bristled. Not if he was going to be rude. "No, I don't. Maybe I'll stay and figure out a way to rescue Tony."

"You'll get captured," Randall said, his voice rising. "You're not making any sense."

"Fine, I won't try to rescue Tony, but the rest makes perfect sense," Mari retorted. "I'll get good meals and have my foot taken care of two more times, and tomorrow I'll meet you in Lisden at Kale's. Just tell me where he lives."

"It's not safe!"

"The Haven is safer than Permandy or Lisden. The three Shifters who left for Ranser won't be back yet, and the two Shifters in town are leaving tomorrow and looking for you, not me. The workhouse isn't fetching me until the day after tomorrow."

"You shouldn't cut it that close."

"I'm not cutting it--"

"Uh, hello, you two?" Lauren said loudly. "I'm really hungry, and I'd like to get going and not get re-captured."

"Oh, sorry." Mari gave Lauren a quick sideways hug. "Go, be safe, and get some food." She threw Randall a defiant look. "I'll see you tomorrow in Lisden around noon." She angled toward Haven, leaving him with a thunderous glower upon his face. Lauren's expression looked worried and tense.

The dirt road to the Haven had turned into a hazardous, gooey path while Mari had been in town. She walked on the firmer edges near the trees, where tufts of sparse grass grew. Maddening, how Randall was acting. Why did he always feel obliged to boss her around like she was eight years younger, rather than only fifteen months? Always thinking he knew better. He probably got it from their father, aka the Critical Dictator. She'd have plenty of time before the workhouse came to fetch her, especially if she left tomorrow right after breakfast. That would be a whole *day* earlier.

She felt guilty about leaving Lauren--especially leaving her with Randall for company--but she wanted one more restful day at the Haven, with the privacy of her own room and the availability of good food. Not to mention the pure bliss of the music wing, and…okay, for a chance of meeting that Sanjen guy again, she had to admit. Was that too much to hope for, one more lovely and romantic dance?

She smiled to herself. It had been pretty cliché-ish that their eyes had locked across the room, like something straight from a romance novel. But she loved the idea of it. The magnetism their attraction drawing them toward each other, merging into a compelling dance. His large dark eyes so solemn and attentive. Yes, Sanjen definitely qualified for tall, dark, and handsome. Add muscular and exotic on top of that.

"131199," she told the gatekeeper at the wrought-iron fence, who threw her slimed robe a disapproving look before unlocking the gate and letting her through.

Inside the Haven, she removed her gunky slipper-shoes and carried them through the halls until she found a white-robed staffperson to ask for another robe and a pair of shoes. A little while later, she sat, clean and dry, slurping a savory stew in the eating area. Her belly gave a happy gurgle, and she gave a prolonged sigh of relief.

No responsibilities or daring rescues to worry about for the rest of the day. She could relax. And tonight, perhaps, she might manage to run into Sanjen.

A movement of white made her look up and into the face of a robed staffperson.

"Are you 131199?" the staffperson inquired.

"Yes," Mari said.

The staffperson gave a curt nod. "You are required to report to the Headmistress' office as soon as it is convenient."

Mari stared as the robed figure swept away. All of a sudden, her stew didn't feel so happy in her stomach. What did the Headmistress want? Hopefully only to scold her for walking too much lately. Or maybe she'd get chewed out for sliming today's robe and shoes. She gulped the rest of her stew and hurried to the dark brown door belonging to the Headmistress.

"Enter," the Headmistress' stiff voice answered to Mari's knock.

Mari slipped inside. The Headmistress sat at a monstrous wooden desk, her back unnaturally straight. The angles of her eyebrows dipped downward, fighting the upward slant caused by the tightness of her hairstyle.

"Sit," the Headmistress ordered.

Feeling like a misbehaved puppy, Mari sat on a chair in front of the desk.

"I hear you've been out again today," the Headmistress said in a clipped voice.

"Yes. I didn't think that was forbidden."

The Headmistress' expression sharpened. "No, but you have been overdoing it, at the expense of your ankle. Last evening the gatekeeper reported a breaking of curfew, and the nurse reported a filthy robe and a swollen ankle. Today I've been informed you've been out in the slime. I don't care where you've been going, but these excursions must halt or you will not be fit for the workhouse in time."

"I won't go out as much," Mari assured her, twisting her hands in her lap. She had to be allowed to leave, or she wouldn't be able to meet up with Randall tomorrow. "Only one more trip, a short one."

"No," the Headmistress said, her voice firm. "You will not go out at all. You are henceforth banned from leaving the Haven grounds. Effective immediately, you will stay inside until you are summoned to be delivered to the workhouse."

Chapter 9

Mari sat motionless, feeling as though the breath had been knocked from her by an invisible fist. Banned. She wouldn't be able to leave in the morning. Her mouth moved, but no sound came out.

"You are dismissed," the Headmistress said with a brief nod toward the door.

"But--you can't--I have to--" Mari said, finding only stray bits of her voice.

"The subject is no longer open to discussion. You will leave now." The Headmistress bent to study a book on her desk. Dismissed. The meeting was over.

Mari shuffled out in a daze, the mental gears in her brain refusing to accept what she'd heard. How could she be banned from leaving? That ruined everything. She'd get sent to the workhouse and assigned to slave labor somewhere, like Stefanie had. What would Randall and Lauren do if she didn't show up tomorrow in Lisden?

She headed for her room, and paced around it like a caged animal. Her watch lay in a pile with her normal clothes and shoes. She looked at them for a minute as she paced, then she sank to her knees in a rush, tossing her watch into her shoes and gathering everything into a roll. No time to dress. She had to escape right now, before the Headmistress informed the gatekeeper that she was banned from leaving.

She flipped her hood up, hurried down the halls, and whipped out the front door of the Haven. The slime rain had slackened, thinning to a pale gray drizzle. At the gate she greeted the gatekeeper.

"Hi, I'd like outside, please." She kept her head down.

From inside his shelter, the gatekeeper rustled a

parchment. "Your number?"

Mari clutched her belongings tighter to her chest, under the cover of her robe sleeves. She'd better not be banned yet. "131199."

"Er, sorry," the gatekeeper said, "you're on the banned list. You can't go out."

Mari swore to herself. Why had she said her real number? "Oh, I'm not sure I said that number right. Are you sure 311399 is banned?"

The gatekeeper sniffed. "That is not a valid number, miss. All numbers begin with 1. You're not allowed outside these gates, 131199. Go back inside."

Blinking back tears of frustration, Mari returned inside. Blast. It had been worth a try, but she'd failed. The idea of being here didn't seem so enjoyable now that she knew she couldn't leave, and knowing she'd be sent to the workhouse.

She hated this dimension.

In her room, she sat on her bed and stared at the blank walls. She'd gotten sucked into such a bad dream. A very *real* bad dream--one where Shifters burned old men's huts, foremen whipped lacerations into workers' backs, and Isolation cell guards gave their prisoners a single piece of stale bread for the day. Who knew what terrible things Stefanie endured at the farm where she stayed.

She kicked her adventure novel across the room. Worst of all, she'd proven Randall right. They shouldn't have separated. She shouldn't have taken a chance. She'd gambled and royally lost.

Unable to stop herself, she felt tears stream down her face and plop onto her robed knees. She'd blown her freedom, and now Randall and Lauren would have to take dangerous risks to rescue her. If they even bothered to try. She was sure Randall would focus on trying to rescue Stefanie first. After all, as a measly little sister she couldn't compete with Stefanie of the silky hair and curvy body. Oh yes, and of the honor roll brain. It was easy to forget that part.

The rest of the afternoon Mari wandered the halls and sat in the garden wing under the cover of a gazebo. She watched the drizzle of slime rain taper off and finally end. The sky, however, remained gray and dismal. After dinner and a trip to the nursing wing, she read more of her adventure novel for lack of anything better to do. She finished the book quite late, closing it with a snap.

Yeah. All very nice for courageous Danielle, with the ends of her story all tied up like neat strings on a pretty package. The heroine triumphs and everyone loves her. Ta-dah. Too bad real life never ended that way. Mari stood up with a growl, yawning and stretching. She blew out her lantern. It was around midnight she guessed, a bit earlier than when she'd seen Sanjen the night before, but he might be dancing in the music room now. She'd go check. She certainly could use a positive ending to this day.

On her way there, she dropped her book off at the library. At the music wing she stood in the entryway, studying the room labels. Calming, Joyous, or Invigorating. That was the question. Which did she need the most? And more importantly, which room would Sanjen most likely visit? The Calming Room would be her first guess.

She shook her head. Crazy. Sanjen probably didn't care if he saw her again, and he was probably long gone, far away. Their dance had been a lovely moment in time that had turned into a lovely memory. She shouldn't get her hopes up. Still, she opened the door of the Calming Room to see if he was there.

He wasn't. Two overweight females danced there, looking like a pair of brown bubbles bouncing in slow motion. She checked the Joyous Room. Not there either.

On the right, the Invigorating Room beckoned to her with its uplifting beat. She stepped to the door with an urgency that bordered on desperation. Yes, that's what she needed right now, whether Sanjen danced there or not. The pulsing, catchy beat grew louder as she opened the door, and the music sounded familiar. *Jaisha.* Tears welled in her eyes. She flung her arms outward to embrace the sounds. Inconceivably, the room played one of her favorite singers, with the throaty melody of Jaisha's voice resonating with the drums and other instruments in the song. Splashes of vibrant color diagonaled across the room's walls-- yellows and violets and greens. The floor whirled with a velvety crimson, like a lava lamp on high speed. The ceiling sparkled with glittering white lights.

She danced, and closed her eyes to shut out the sight of the three other robed figures in the room, imagining herself at a school dance instead. She imagined the gawky, self-conscious teen boys shuffling near the walls. The shy girls with fawn eyes trailing their dreamguys across the room, watching them dance with someone else. The brash, self-assured boys making the rounds with the prettiest girls. She imagined the cheerleaders, the preppies, the populars. The pained souls who did not belong to any category.

Like her, the new girl. Out of it, on the fringes, not fitting well into any groove.

After a while two of the dancing inhabitants left the room. Mari danced on. She knew it probably neared one o'clock and she should sleep, but she hated for this feeling of pseudo-normalcy to end. In a few more minutes, however, the songs of Jaisha drifted from the room, replaced by a lively but wordless beat. Mari stopped dancing, her energy suddenly spent, the spell broken. Her mood plummeted.

She sighed and walked out of the room. In the entryway, she looked toward the Calming Room. Did she need that room in order to get to sleep? Maybe. She could at least check for Sanjen once more. She stepped over with pinpricks of anticipation tingling down her arms and legs, and opened the door.

Empty of dancers.

Disappointment surged through her. And yet, the soft music rose and fell in waves like the ocean, sliding up and down invisible coastlines, splashing onto unseen rocks. The cries of distant seagulls layered over the waves. Very nice. She'd relax here before she went to her room.

Sitting on a bench covered by a blue woolen, she let the music soak into her. She sank into a mindless slump, trying not to think of anything. The opposite wall looked like blue-tinged emptiness. She rested, becoming empty like the wall. A faint shifting noise that didn't quite fit in with the sounds of the ocean made her turn her head.

Sanjen had come in. He stood poised a few feet into the room, studying her. He hesitated a few seconds before walking over, his expression guarded. His thick dark lashes made his eyes appear outlined, as with black eyeliner.

"Hi," she said to him. She felt as tentative as he looked.

"Hi," he said, after a brief pause. "Tired of dancing?"

"Yes," Mari said, then gave herself a swift mental kick. If he'd wanted to dance with her, she'd just eliminated the opportunity. "I danced in the Invigorating Room for a while, then came here to relax."

"It's a good place to relax, especially for travelers like me." Sanjen sat on the bench, a careful two feet away.

Mari sneaked a look at his profile as he leaned against the wall. Nice. A strong profile, very masculine. But he seemed so cautious. Wasn't he used to talking with females? She blew out a deep sigh and focused on the opposite blue wall again.

"Rough day?" Sanjen asked. His words came easier, as though he found it less demanding to talk without eye contact.

"Yes," Mari said. "A lousy day. That slopping slime rain, the stinking mines. I got into an argument with my brother, and those blasted Shifters roaming around town...." She trailed off, overwhelmed by the horridness of her situation.

"My uncle doesn't live in this landscape, but he's been a Shifter for twelve years."

"Oh, sorry." She threw him a panicked glance. Oops. And here she'd thought Shifter-bashing was a safe subject in Permandy. She'd better watch what she said. "So people actually decide to become Shifters, and they're not born that way?"

He gave an amused grunt. "Yes. They realize there has to be something more to life than these bleak landscapes. My uncle joined and began training when I was eight, so I learned a lot about being one."

Aha. A perfect information source if she ever heard one. "Most people don't know much about them," she said. "I sure don't. It's confusing. Like, supposedly there's some Portal where newcomers come in from another dimension or landscape, right?"

Sanjen shifted to meet her gaze. "Right. Except technically, there's a difference between dimensions and landscapes. Newcomers come from another dimension, called the Mainworld. Our dimension here is divided into millions of landscapes. This landscape, with Permandy and the surrounding villages, is merely one of those millions of landscapes."

Mari let that information soak into her brain for a minute. "So the newcomers happen to pop through the Portal from this Mainworld dimension one day, into one of these millions of landscapes?"

"It's not that random. They travel only to one specific landscape, the landscape they have composed from their own dreams and nightmares. Call it ironic, or a poetic justice of sorts."

"Composed from their dreams and nightmares?" Mari echoed, her heart pounding faster.

"Yes," Sanjen said, running a hand over his short-cropped hair, ruffling it like ebony feathers. "Made up of the things the Mainworlder adores, and of the things he or she is most terrified. For instance, the Builder of our landscape loves music, dancing, and brilliant blue skies. He or she loathes rustic lifestyles, and fears spiders and Executioners who enforce curfews. Among other things."

Mari's mind reeled. "You mean, this landscape with Permandy and Lisden and everything, it's made up from someone's mind, someone who lives in the Mainworld?"

Sanjen nodded. "That's what the Shifters believe. As you are aware, most everyday people don't believe it."

A clammy shudder crawled over her. She didn't need a hundred guesses to know who the Builder of this landscape was. It was her creation, all of it--her old nightmare with the Executioner, the hideous vampire spiders, as well as the slime rain and the ravenous Pit that consumed rocks. No wonder the Invigorating Room played Jaisha, and the skies appeared like a Maxfield Parrish painting at sunset. No wonder the neon-pink flowers smelled like Grandma Stratton's perfume--

She raised her hands, pressing them over her face. "Oh, wow. That's too mind-boggling to imagine, let alone believe," she murmured.

"Yes, it's an overwhelming concept," Sanjen agreed. "But take heart. At least life in this landscape is somewhat livable. Other landscapes are much, much worse, because of the severe fears that have built them."

She dropped her hands. "How would Shifters know that other landscapes are worse?"

"Shifters can travel between landscapes."

"But not to the Mainworld?"

"No. They need a Mainworlder to take them there, through the Portal."

"How does the Portal do that?" Mari asked, hardly daring to hope for an answer.

"A triangle marks the Portal. Touching activates it. It glows, the Mainworlders travel," Sanjen said. "So the theory goes--I haven't ever seen it, of course."

Right on. Touch the triangle and go, easy to remember.

Mari frowned. "So why do the Shifters race around ruthlessly capturing newcomers? Why don't they just ask them to travel back to the Mainworld with them? You know, be polite about it."

To her surprise, Sanjen gave a slight chuckle and a stiff half-smile. "As my uncle used to say, 'it's better to act first and ask questions later.' Shifters only know when a Portal has been activated. They don't know how much knowledge the Mainworlders have about returning or the negative consequences of bringing someone from this dimension back to the Mainworld."

"What are the consequences?" Mari asked, more a faint breath than words.

"A blank slate. Not only is the landscape of that Mainworlder destroyed, but so is his or her ability to have dreams--good or bad--while sleeping."

Mari stared at Sanjen. Did that mean a Mainworlder like her wouldn't be able to dream anymore, and that particular portion of her mind would be wiped out? She suppressed a shudder, and reminded herself to breathe. "Do all the people in a landscape die when a landscape gets destroyed?"

"No, everything simply disappears after twenty-four hours. Extinguished like a candle flame. Once alive and existing, then gone."

"Oh." Mari thought of Pod's friendly gaping grin, Lynia's gentle smile. The Magistrate, all the soldiers, the townspeople. The two giggling girls with the butter churn. And Sanjen. If she or the others brought a Shifter through the Portal with them, Sanjen would vanish into nothingness. "That's really sad," she whispered.

"I suppose," Sanjen said, his voice casual. "There are much worse ways to die than suddenly ceasing to exist."

Silent, Mari looked full into his face, trying to memorize it.

Sanjen didn't turn away. His head tilted a fraction. "Do you live here in Permandy?"

"Uh, for now," Mari said. "My life is such a mess. I'd wanted to go stay with my brother in Lisden tomorrow, but that didn't work out." Yeah, so much for that plan. She wished somehow that Sanjen could help her escape the Haven, hide her in a suitcase or a duffel bag or whatever antiquated way people around here carried things. She felt a pang of distress as Sanjen unfolded into a graceful, powerful stand. Was he leaving?

"I must return to my room and sleep," Sanjen said with a slight bow. "The morning comes soon." He turned to go, then swung back. "If you are ever in need of a place to stay near Lisden, Mari, you may go to my cottage. Go through Lisden, turn left at the fork. The first cottage is mine. I travel a lot and am not always there, but you're welcome to use it if you're stranded by the curfew or something."

Mari stood. "Thank you." She couldn't muster up a smile. He didn't smile either, and he'd spoken with difficulty. Maybe he wasn't used to giving invitations like this. Or maybe, like her, he suspected she'd never be able to take him up on his offer. They'd each go their separate ways in the morning. She to the workhouse, he to Lisden or his travels.

They'd never see each other again.

"Have a good tomorrow," he said. He gave her a farewell nod, and walked from the room.

Chapter 10

The following morning Mari sat in the garden wing on the grass, watching birds fly overhead, and counting grasshoppers that leaped across her legs. The sky glowed bright and blue, as though the slime rain of the day before had never happened. Her conversation with Sanjen played over and over in her mind.

Her fault. This entire horrid landscape had been built by her fears and insecurities. She pushed up her right robe sleeve and fingered the welted mark seared onto her forearm. A triangle, exactly like the Portal marking on the cave wall. Divided into five smaller triangles. Did that mean one triangle represented each of them--her, Randall, Lauren, Stefanie, and Tony? The triangle had glowed when she'd touched it. If all five of them had touched an inner triangle, simultaneously, would they have been transported back to their own dimension, right after they'd arrived?

How frustrating. None of this mess would've happened. They'd be home right now, enjoying the last days of their winter vacation. Mari snorted. Or, more like it, she'd be working at the pizzeria, grating cheese and waiting tables. She hated waiting tables, even with the lure of tips. The whole customer service bit wasn't her thing.

But she'd rather wait tables than be here in this nightmare dimension.

She flicked loose grass from her robe, Sanjen's face materializing again in her memory. He seemed more educated and refined than most people in this village. Was that his Shifter uncle's influence? But then, odd exceptions did exist in Permandy. The Magistrate, for instance, and the Headmistress and the nurse. Lynia. Even the Haven staff and gatekeeper talked less rustic.

That was fortunate. It helped her blend in better, and helped prevent others--like Sanjen--from spotting her as a Mainworlder. Would Sanjen turn her over to his uncle if he knew she was a Mainworlder? She hoped he wouldn't, but she had walked a thin, risky line last night.

Sanjen had said Shifters traveled between landscapes in this dimension. Maybe that was how they'd obtained guns, from a more advanced landscape. And probably why the Magistrate had asked Mari and the others if they'd gotten their flashlights and modern clothing from another landscape. Although the Magistrate had said other dimensions *or* landscapes; he apparently didn't know the technical difference between the two.

She shuddered, thinking of the vampire spiders and the Executioner. If she'd been born in this dimension, she might've considered joining the Shifters as Sanjen's uncle had. A chance at escape or a different life, even if slim, would be tempting. Speaking of which, she hoped she could escape from the workhouse tomorrow, or from whatever place the workhouse sent her.

Footsteps crunched along the path. She looked up to see Lynia's thin figure approaching through the garden. Mari smiled as Lynia caught sight of her.

"I'm glad to see you before I leave tomorrow," Lynia said, sitting down beside her. "I enjoyed our talk the other day."

"I'm leaving tomorrow morning too," Mari said. "I wish I wasn't."

Lynia clenched her bird-fragile hands tight in her lap. "Me too. I'm grateful for the wealth and vast size of our farm and cottage, but Gand, my husband, is a big man, and he doesn't realize his own force with the strap or his fists."

His fists. Mari swallowed, hard. She wondered how many bruises were covered by Lynia's monk robe. "Can't you leave him and run away somewhere? Anywhere's got to be better than living like that."

Lynia shook her head. "I'm afraid. I've never been out on my own. I wouldn't know where to begin, or if I could provide for myself."

"What about the workhouse?" Mari asked. "Or is that really hard work, and too much like being a slave?"

Lynia gave a soft laugh. "I'm nearly a slave now. Packing water, tending to the goats and chickens, scrubbing laundry, cooking Gand's food. It wouldn't be much different than the last five years. But Gand says I'm not very good at my chores. I slosh when I carry buckets from the stream, and sometimes I scorch the biscuits. No wonder he beats me." She fell silent, her gaze dropping to her lap.

"I bet you'd do fine," Mari exclaimed. "Gand sounds way too picky. I'm being sent to the workhouse in the morning. Why don't you come with me?"

Lynia's head jerked up, her pale brown eyes wide. "Truly, you are going to the workhouse?"

"Yes. But I don't know where I'll get assigned. We might get separated."

Nodding, Lynia pondered that. "Yes, but it would help my confidence if you accompanied me at first. I could ask the Headmistress to prepare Departure Papers to leave Gand officially." She stared glassy-eyed at a bright patch of yellow flowers, as though an alternative future lay there.

Mari reached over and patted Lynia's hand. "Decide what you think is best, but I think you'd be happier somewhere else. Or at least, not any unhappier."

"True," Lynia said. A slow smile spread across her face. "What would I be losing?" She leaped up from the grass. "I'm off to sign Departure Papers. Thank you, Mari!"

"You go, girl," Mari said, then laughed at the perplexed look Lynia threw over her shoulder as she hurried away.

That afternoon, following the mid-day meal, Mari connected with Lynia again in the garden wing. They chatted for a while, then visited the music wing for a joint dance in the Joyous Room. Lynia's mood seemed to become more joyous than Mari's. Lynia's papers had been signed and a copy sent off to her husband Gand. Her future held promise.

Mari, on the other hand, couldn't quite shake a weighty sense of foreboding, and a sharp desperation to escape.

The next morning Mari nabbed a quick breakfast and dressed in her jeans, powder-blue top, and normal shoes. After stashing her ring, watch, and earrings in her jeans pocket, she tossed her robe in the laundry bin and walked to the nursing wing for her last ointment session. To her relief, her ankle looked fine after a day's rest. The nurse pronounced her healed, and Mari walked out to the main entryway. There Lynia already waited, wearing a tan peasant dress with a dingy apron tied at the waist.

Lynia's mouth fell open as she looked Mari up and down. "You're wearing an odd set of clothing. My goodness, trousers--like men wear. Where did you get those?"

"I'm a newcomer," Mari said. "Where I come from, this is what we wear. Do you still want to be seen with me?"

"I'm not worried," Lynia said with a shrug. "Folks will be staring at you, not me."

Mari gave a half-hearted smile. Oh yeah, that was

reassuring.

The Headmistress emerged from her office room like a white-robed specter, and scrutinized them coolly. "Go wait out by the gate," she ordered. "You are both hereby dismissed from the Haven. The wagon from the workhouse will be here soon."

Lynia took a deep breath and flipped her long braid behind her shoulder before they walked out the door and across the courtyard. Mari chewed on her lip. If there was an opportunity to escape once she got outside the gates, would she take it? She wanted to, but she didn't want to abandon Lynia. Blast.

They waited in the sun, with the greasy stench of the nearby mining yard making Mari feel nauseous. By now, Randall and Lauren would've guessed something had happened to her. Who knew what they'd thought or done when she hadn't shown up in Lisden yesterday. Both of them seemed to do well at planning rather than panicking, though.

Mari heard the wagon rumbling and creaking up the rutted road before she saw it. In a few minutes a sturdy horse clopped up to the gate, pulling a low-sided wagon. The driver, a big man with a goatskin vest and a scruffy beard, called out for the horse to halt. He grabbed a pile of metal with a rattling clank and jumped down almost before the wagon had halted. Mari's stomach dropped to her toes when she realized what he held in his hands.

Shackles. So much for any escape thoughts. She hoped she wouldn't be shackled and chained at the place she'd be working. Was Stefanie chained at her farm? Randall hadn't said.

The gatekeeper bustled over to open the gate. "These two are the ones you want," he said to the bearded man, pointing at Mari and Lynia.

The man lumbered up and clasped small shackles around their wrists. He pulled on the chain connected to the shackles, drawing them to the wagon. "Come along," he said.

"Oh no," Lynia said, looking at her wrist in dismay, "this isn't necessary, sir. I'm volunteering to go to the workhouse--I won't try to escape."

"Got my orders, miss," the man drawled. "I treat everyone the same." He fastened the chain to an iron ring behind the wagon seat, and motioned for them to climb up. They exchanged anxious looks, and clambered inside.

"We can't work with shackles on," Mari said, low. "I bet they'll be taken off once we get placed somewhere."

"I hope so," Lynia said. "Although it'd still be better than living with Gand."

They fell silent as they set off, bumping over the ruts of the road. The boards of the wagon scraped against Mari's spine, and the shackle hung cold and heavy on her wrist. The golden road glittered once more in the sun as the driver followed it into Permandy. Mari darted nervous glances around the marketplace. She hoped the Shifters had left for their Fortress yesterday or the day before, as planned, because here she sat in this open wagon, looking like an obvious Mainworlder. She wished the Haven would've let her keep wearing her robe.

The wagon turned left at the candlemaker's table and drove on, passing the Magistrate's building and stopping in front of the long workhouse building. The bearded man jumped down as a woman appeared in the doorway. It was the same woman with the lined, hard face whom Mari had asked about Stefanie.

"Ah, there you are," the woman said to the driver.

"I've received word that Marva at the Permandy Inn has taken a fall and hurt her hip. The Innkeeper requests at least one more permanent worker. Even if Marva recovers, there is really more work there than one person can handle." She walked over and surveyed Mari and Lynia, giving a doubtful sniff. "We'd better send both of these gals. Together they might make one good worker."

Lynia made an indignant noise, and Mari threw her a cautioning look.

"I'll take 'em right over," the driver said, climbing back onto the driver's platform.

"Wait," the workhouse woman said, frowning at Mari. "The dark-haired one has inappropriate clothing for working in a public place. We don't want any trouble with the townsfolk or Shifters. Let me send along a blouse and a skirt." She disappeared inside.

Lynia leaned toward Mari. "Should I show her my Departure Papers?" she whispered.

"I don't think it would change anything," Mari said. "You could show the Innkeeper, though."

Lynia nodded. "I'm glad we're getting placed together."

"I know, that's great," Mari said, as the workhouse woman returned with a long-sleeved tan blouse and a long brown skirt. The woman tossed the clothing into Mari's lap.

"Off with the both of you," the woman said. "Work hard and earn your keep. You'll get food and lodging for your labors, which you should be grateful for."

Mari repressed a snort. Slaves got food and lodging. And that's all they'd be. Slaves.

The driver set the horse into motion again. They headed south toward the Haven and turned onto a side road. The Permandy Inn sat hunched like a foul creature not far from the golden road, all cracked boards and moss, cockeyed wooden shutters and rusty hinges. Chickens and geese scattered like feathered buckshot as the wagon lumbered up to the front porch.

The driver dismounted and unfastened the chain. He held one end like a leash and indicated the Inn with a jerk of his head. "This way," he ordered. "Innkeeper's in the kitchen, most likely."

Mari gathered the peasant clothing with her free hand and clambered down with Lynia. They followed the driver around to the back, past a large scraggly garden and through a roofed porch area. An overpowering smell of boiling cabbage, smoldering firewood, and something indefinably rank hit Mari's nose like a solid wall. The narrow kitchen assaulted her senses with a garish mixture of color and clutter, filled with battered iron pots, assorted bowls, a pile of skinned rabbits, a cooking area with a wide open fireplace, and a muddy tumble of potatoes and turnips.

A hefty woman muttered over the pile of rabbits, while a trim, dark-haired man faced away from them by the cooking pit, stirring the pungent cabbage mixture in a huge pot hanging from a rod. The man swung the pot back over the fire and wiped his hands on a cloth tucked into his trousers waistband.

"Sir," the driver addressed the man. "I've brought two girls from the workhouse. I hope they'll serve you well."

The man turned to face them, and Mari let out a startled yelp. The man, his black hair tinged with gray, wore the trousers and simple tunic-shirt that every other male in Permandy wore. But his face belonged to an efficient businessman, one that prided himself on practical decisions and efficiency. She recognized the shrewd blue eyes, the furrowed brow, and the demanding mouth. This was someone who didn't take kindly to hesitations, laziness, or displays of tears.

This man belonged to another dimension. This man was her father.

Chapter 11

Mari's emotions seared her, her shock making her arms and legs tremble. She stared at the Innkeeper, unable to fathom the sight of her father here, in this dimension. "Dad?" she croaked.

He squinted at her, looked her up and down. "Don't mumble, girl," he said brusquely. "And change into your proper clothes--don't stand there clutching them like a frightened mouse. Driver, release this one so she can dress."

"Yes, sir," the bearded man said. He set to work on Mari's shackle. Mari's eyes flicked to the Innkeeper. He didn't seem to know her. If this wasn't her real father, he was an extremely convincing copy.

"I--I have Departure Papers," Lynia spoke up, drawing a copy from her apron pocket. "I've come here willingly, having left my farm with Gand McFee."

The Innkeeper's dark eyebrows shot upward. "Are you mad, woman? I've heard of Gand McFee. He owns one of the largest farms in the valley."

Lynia's chin jutted out. "Nevertheless, I've left him. I will work for you now."

The Innkeeper grunted. "As you wish. Let's see how you do. Since you're here willingly, you will perform the outside duties, and you--" he gave a terse nod toward Mari, "will perform the inside duties where we can keep you in our sights. Penna, my cook, will tell you both what those duties are." He spun and left the kitchen through an inner doorway.

Penna, the hefty woman by the rabbits, tossed a sullen look at the inner doorway. "I ain't in no position to be mindin' scrawny new workers like some fool nursemaid," she grumbled.

The driver chuckled, released Lynia, and retreated

out the back door with a clanking of empty chains and shackles. Mari rubbed her wrist where the shackle band had been, and slipped the blouse and skirt over her own clothes. When she escaped, she didn't want to have to worry about finding her real clothes.

Lynia faced the cook. "What are my chores, ma'am?"

Penna put her hands on her round hips with a blustery exhale. "You'll be tendin' the garden, haulin' water from the creek, feedin' pigs and chickens, milkin' goats, and washin' linens." She rattled off a few more chores, then added, "But first, fetch some creek water so this other little gal can get to work on the spuds and turnips. Buckets are on the back porch."

"Yes, ma'am." In a flash, Lynia crossed the kitchen and whipped out the back door.

"You," Penna said to Mari, "will do kitchen work. Cuttin', cleanin', and stirrin'. You'll also be servin' guests their grub and brew. And straightenin' the rooms upstairs after the guests leave."

Mari had to struggle to keep her lip from curling. Great. Not only would she have to work in this filthy kitchen, but she'd have to act as waitress and motel maid too. The first chance she saw to escape, she was taking it.

Penna handed her a knife. "The loaves of bread on that table have cooled. Slice 'em up. If someone yells for more ale, get it from over there." She pointed to a lineup of battered casks with spigots.

Mari nodded and moved to the work table. While cutting the coarse bread into slices, she peered through the doorway into the serving hall. She saw a scattering of crude wooden tables and benches, and a rough floor strewn with apple cores, crusts of bread, and chicken bones. A large chipped mirror hung on the wall near the

114

stairs. Three men slumped at one table, slurping from thick metal mugs and erupting into periodic, ear-splitting guffaws. The whole serving room stank like beer, strong and sour in her nostrils, as though it soaked every piece of wood in the place. She didn't know which smelled worse, the kitchen or the serving hall.

She cringed as something beetle-like scuttled across the floor by her feet and disappeared under a grain sack. Ugh. No wonder the Shifters hated to stay here. Poor Tony had also stayed here, after the Shifters had captured him.

"More ale!" bellowed a voice from the serving hall.

Hesitant, Mari edged into the hall and over to the table of men. A red-faced man held out his mug. She took it gingerly, and caught sight of the Innkeeper coming down the stairs.

"What's your problem, girl?" the Innkeeper demanded.

"Well, I'm only sixteen," Mari said. "I can't serve--" She broke off as the Innkeeper's eyes narrowed. "Never mind." Okay, okay. She'd pour the ale, since apparently in this dimension regular liquor-serving rules didn't apply. She hurried into the kitchen away from the Innkeeper's intense scrutiny. It gave her a chill, the way he looked like her father, ready to launch into one of his lectures.

She filled the mug with a cloudy, yellow-brown liquid from one of the casks, and delivered it to the red-faced man. When she got back to the kitchen, Lynia had returned and was pouring two buckets of water into a large wooden tub that sat on the floor.

"Now scrub and chop those spuds and turnips," Penna directed Mari, hacking at a rabbit carcass with a huge butcher knife.

"Okay," Mari said, hurrying to finish the bread

slicing. Flies buzzed around her head, and she swatted at them. They kept landing on the bread, looking like dark knots of six-legged raisins. Gross. She hoped she wouldn't be given this bread to eat, later on. But she knew it was probably a feeble hope.

Lynia dashed outside again. Done with the bread slicing, Mari grabbed a turnip, broke off the green top, and kneeled on the floor to wash it at the tub. She'd rubbed it semi-clean and was reaching for another one when she noticed the Innkeeper standing in the doorway. With a frown, he grabbed a wooden-handled brush from the clutter on the counter and tossed it down to her.

"Brushes do a better job scrubbing than bare hands," he advised. "Plus, it'd make more sense if you'd dump those vegetables in the water to soak while you scrub the others. Not dabbing at them one by one. Use your brain, girl. Don't waste valuable time being inefficient." He pivoted and exited the kitchen.

Unexplainably, Mari gasped in pain, sucking in her breath, feeling like she'd been slugged in the shoulder-- hard. Water sloshed from the tub as she sprawled across it, confused and blinking. She clutched her shoulder, tears streaming down her face, her breathing coming in irregular bursts.

What in the world had just happened?

The Innkeeper hadn't touched her, hadn't moved a hand or a foot, and yet she'd felt a solid punch land on her right shoulder. Had she missed seeing his foot kick her? She didn't think so. He'd been over three feet from her, much too far to kick and withdraw his foot that fast. Worst of all, he'd sounded exactly like her father, giving one of his demeaning lectures on being practical and efficient.

Shaken, she straightened and picked up the brush.

She scrubbed at the vegetables until they'd all been cleaned, keeping a wary eye out for the Innkeeper. After she chopped the turnips and potatoes, Penna directed her to stir the stew, and to sweep. As the day wore on and edged into the late afternoon, the Inn began to fill up, with the guests pounding on the tables and roaring for meals and more of the murky ale. Mari sprinted back and forth between the kitchen and the serving hall, sweating. Lynia appeared in the kitchen with a bucket of goat's milk, finding a place to put it without bothering Penna to ask where. Mari envied her self-assuredness.

She left for the serving hall with four mugs of ale.

"Where's my dinner?" demanded a brown-cloaked man with a droopy mustache, glaring at Mari as she deposited the ale at a table near his. "I want to eat before I go up to my room."

Mari swore under her breath. She'd forgotten to serve that guy, had gotten sidetracked.

"Sorry, I'll get it." Mari ran into the kitchen, almost colliding with the Innkeeper. "Sorry!" she cried again, chagrined. She piled roasted rabbit and chunks of boiled cabbage, potatoes, and turnips onto a platter. As she set the platter down to add a slice of bread, a beetle-like shape zipped over her wrist and onto the platter, coming to a leggy rest in the middle of a potato chunk.

She shrieked, jumping back. What the blazes was that? It was huge, over two inches long, standing there with spindly legs and antennas twitching. Perched right on the food. Nausea rose to her throat.

The Innkeeper stamped over. "What's the matter?"

Words failed her. She pointed at the bug on the platter, her stomach churning.

"It's just a stupid cockroach," the Innkeeper snapped. He snatched up the bug and flung it onto the floor, mashing it with a sickening crunch under his boot. "Stop overreacting. If you fall apart over every little problem, how are you ever going to handle the big problems? Now go serve that food before it gets cold." He stalked away.

Mari reeled sideways, feeling a slamming impact as though she'd been punched again, this time in the face. She clutched her jaw, gulping and gasping. Tears sprang to her eyes. She'd heard that lecture before. *Quit overreacting, Mari Leigh Stratton,* her father had said to her on numerous occasions. *Stop making something out of nothing.*

She smeared tears from her face. The rowdy din of the men in the next room seemed to mock her, overly loud and full of boisterous laughter. She bit down on her lip to keep it steady while she walked out and served the platter. As she passed the mirror by the stairs to fetch more ale, she glanced into it.

She halted, gaping. A wicked purplish bruise had already appeared on the side of her face where the phantom punch had landed. She touched it, wincing.

"Ale!" the man in the corner hollered.

She fled to the kitchen with the mug she held, her lungs heaving and trying to find air. Her trembling fingers could barely turn the handle on the cask spigot. She didn't know how this weird phenomenon was happening, but she didn't like it. Somehow, the Innkeeper's *words* were hitting her, hurting her. She'd be bruised from head to toe in a few days if she didn't escape.

Wishing she had some ice, she took the man his ale.

The rest of the evening passed, nightmare-like. By the time all the ale drinkers and Inn guests had either staggered home or up the stairs to their rooms, Mari's entire body felt limp with exhaustion. Lynia came in the back door as the sun hovered near the horizon and Mari finished washing the last pot. Alone in the serving hall, Mari and Lynia ate bread, rabbit, and vegetables at an empty table. Mari tried not to think of buzzing flies or antenna-waving cockroaches while she chewed. She leaned closer to Lynia.

"I'm escaping as soon as I can," she said. "I want to go to Lisden, where my brother is."

A sad, sweet smile flitted across Lynia's face. "Of course, if you must. I'll miss you, but I think I'll do all right here. It's hard work, but at least no one hits me."

"Yes, that's definitely good," Mari said. She touched the side of her aching face and sighed. "I need a cool, wet cloth to put on this bruise." A wet cloth would have to do, since ice or freezers didn't exist in this ridiculous dimension.

Lynia's eyebrows gathered in confusion. "What bruise?"

"The one on my face," Mari said, pointing. "I bet I have one on my shoulder, too." It felt tender and bruised. She pushed her blouse aside to check, and frowned. Hmm. Nothing on her shoulder.

"Your face isn't bruised, Mari," Lynia said. "It might hurt, but it looks fine."

"What?" Mari got up and walked to the mirror. She stared. A huge purplish bruise covered most of one jaw. Out of curiosity, she checked her shoulder in the mirror, and her frown deepened. The mirror showed a mottled, purplish-black bruise on her shoulder. But nothing showed when she looked down at her shoulder.

Only the mirror showed her bruises. Freaky. Way freaky.

How could the Innkeeper's words make invisible bruises like this? Since this dimension featured her fears, and the Innkeeper acted like her father, it had to mean something. The pain was certainly real. Did it mean invisible or hidden abuse? Her real father had never laid a hand on her, but she knew she carried his bruising words around with her all the time. Was he affecting her more than she realized?

She didn't know, but one thing she knew for certain. Though she hadn't gotten a chance today, tomorrow she would try to check out of this Inn, permanently.

Mari awoke on a straw pallet next to Lynia, stiff and groggy. Penna's hard leathered toe nudged her in the ribs.

"Up, the both of you. Dawn's almost here, chores are a-waitin'." Penna waddled away.

Lynia stretched and shoved her pallet under the stairs. Mari did the same, adding her bedraggled hunk of musty blanket, and the morning began in a blur of gummy porridge and cracked bowls, stringy ham and belligerent guests. Breakfast duties accomplished, the Innkeeper sent Mari upstairs to straighten the beds and rooms--and tend to the chamber pots.

Standing downstairs on the porch later on, Mari held her breath, gagging as she lined up another chamber pot for Lynia to empty. She'd found an old rag to handle the pots with, but her hands felt filthy and contaminated. She watched Lynia scurry across the yard with a pot, and shook her head. Lynia's thin body looked fragile, but boy, could that girl churn out the chores.

Behind her, the sizzling pop of the wood in the cooking pit sounded like gunshot. Chickens cackled and flurried across the yard. Lynia bent to hurl the contents of the pot into a nearby trench, and Mari glanced around. She should leave, now! While the Innkeeper stomped around upstairs and Penna stood absorbed with whatever disgusting goo she'd begun to concoct for the midday meal, it was time to make a run for it.

Mari leaped off the porch and ran hard, darting through one end of the straggly garden, aiming for the back edge of the property. She rushed past of the last row of carrots, when something snagged her feet, tripping her and sending her plunging face-first into the dirt. A cloud of dust flurried around her. She wheezed, her lungs trying to recuperate from the force of her fall.

Her head spun. She rattled off a string of murky swear words and thrashed into a sitting position, reaching to free her feet from whatever had tripped her. It felt like thick metal, wrapped around both ankles. Her fingers found the feel of a pair of unyielding metal shackles attached to a long chain, at the same time her eyes saw that nothing was there.

Absolutely nothing.

"No, no, no!" she cried. How could this be? Was this incredible insanity related to the phantom punches and invisible bruises, and would she be stuck at this Inn forever?

She got up, aching all over, and hobbled back to the porch. On the steps she bent and felt her ankles again. Gone. The phantom shackles had vanished. She growled and went back inside. Talk about the outer limits of insanity. Did the shackles only show up at the edges of the Inn property, to keep her contained?

There had to be a way to escape. She'd find it. Soon.

The menu of the day turned out to be a mutton stew with carrots and dumplings. Mari slaved all morning, chopping, stirring, and knocking cockroaches off the counter with a wooden spoon. A sparse luncheon crowd filtered in to sip ale and order bowls of stew. She skirted the Innkeeper in the serving hall and served a balding man a mug of cloudy ale.

The front door opened. Blinding sun shot into the dim hall, and all thoughts of mysterious punches, invisible shackles, and malfunctioning mirrors evaporated from Mari's mind. With boots and swirling black cloaks clasped with gold triangles, four Shifters entered the Inn.

Chapter 12

The loud conversation and laughter in the room ebbed as the other guests caught sight of the Shifters. A graying, stocky Shifter threw out an arrogant call for ale, his voice harsh and grating.

Bierce.

Mari sidled into the kitchen, her heart going into turbo-speed, her blood pumping like wildfire through her body. Shifters! They'd spot her as a Mainworlder faster than any peasant would. She rolled up the legs of her jeans as far as she could, so they wouldn't accidentally show under her skirt. Luckily, she was petite with short legs, and the skirt hung lower than it might've on other girls. With fumbling fingers, she removed her shoes and socks. Throwing a glance at Penna, who was kneading bread dough, she jammed her shoes and socks behind one of the ale casks.

She grabbed four mugs and filled them, frowning down at her blouse. The blue of her top underneath made the tan look darker. No time to take it off. Hopefully, it'd be okay.

She padded out with the mugs, two in each hand. The Shifters sat at a table by themselves, huddled like dark vultures, muttering to each other. She forced herself to walk over. Surprised, she discovered that one of them was a woman with short hair. Mari tried to keep her eyes off the triangles on their cloaks, relieved that none of them seemed to be paying her much attention.

Until she served the last Shifter, who wore a trim goatee. When she clunked his drink in front of him, his hand shot out and grasped her wrist. "We didn't see you in here a few days ago," he said, looking her over. "Are you new?" His fingers constricted like a claw, his grip strong.

The other three Shifters turned their focus upon her. She felt exposed, x-rayed. Surely the goateed Shifter could feel her pulse racing under his fingers.

She forced herself to shrug. "Not really. I've been around. My father's the Innkeeper." She nodded at the Innkeeper as he strode across the room and received payment coins from the balding man she'd just served. He looked efficient and in control of his sorry, dilapidated Inn.

Bierce twisted to look, then grunted. "Yeah, he looks like your father."

The goateed Shifter's eyes roamed Mari's face. "Yes. Same blue eyes, ebony hair, slight build. Your mouth is curvier though--much more feminine." His eyes glittered, and his free hand slipped up to stroke Mari's hand with his fingertips.

"Zander," Bierce growled, "stop ogling and pawing the infants, and get your mind on the task at hand."

"I like 'em young," Zander protested, releasing Mari's wrist. "Besides, I'm not ancient as you, you old goat."

"W-would you like some dinner?" Mari's words came out breathless. "Mutton stew with carrots and dumplings today." Her legs wobbled. She hoped she wouldn't collapse in a heap on the floor before she had a chance to retreat.

"Sure, bring four," Bierce said. "Now beat it."

Mari rushed to the kitchen, kicking herself in the mental pants for suggesting dinner. Now she'd have to go back to the table at least two more times. In the steamy, rancid kitchen, she loaded two large bowls with care, checking for cockroaches. Taking a huge breath to calm herself, she returned to the table.

"Maybe we shouldn't have left him to babysit the

124

Mainworlder," the woman Shifter was saying. "We could use his help here in Permandy."

"He stays as a guard, Morris," Bierce said, leaning back a little as Mari placed a heaping bowl in front of him. "We're not risking losing the one Mainworlder we have. But I tell you, something's fishy. All three girls were supposedly sent to Ranser, and no one on the wharf knew anything. It doesn't add up."

"You think the Magistrate pulled one over on us?" Zander asked, flashing Mari a quick smile as she placed the second bowl in front of him.

"It's starting to look that way," Bierce said, his grating voice taking on a harder edge.

Mari hurried back into the kitchen to fill another pair of bowls, her mind spinning. So the fifth Shifter had stayed at their Fortress to guard Tony…and if the Shifters confirmed that the Magistrate had lied, it wouldn't be long until they tracked her and Stefanie down.

The Innkeeper materialized by the soup pot, glancing down at her in annoyance. "Why aren't there shoes and stockings on your feet, girl?" he chided. "This is an Inn, not a cottage where you can gallivant around dressed however you please. I'll not have you being lazy about your appearance here, do you understand?"

"Yes, sir." She set the bowls down with a frown, bracing herself for a delayed phantom punch as he turned away. Whatever. She didn't have time for his perfectionism and criticism right now. She had more important things on her mind. Her shoes had to stay off for a while, and laziness had nothing to do with it. With a sigh, she waited for the pain of the invisible blow.

The punch never came. Amazed, she hefted the soup bowls and carted them into the serving hall. Did the Innkeeper's words only bruise her when she *let* them affect her?

Mari approached the Shifters' table as the fourth Shifter spoke. "I say we should start checking the arm of every boy who looks under twenty," he said. "Even if the girls really are in Ranser or on a ship, that other boy from the mining yard is still loose."

"I agree, Markus," Bierce said around a mouthful of stew. "After we pay our little social visit to the Magistrate, we'll start with the north end of Permandy and work our way south. We'll stay here at the Inn tonight. Tomorrow we'll continue our search, and around mid-day we'll reach Lisden. I bet we'll scoop up the girls that way, too."

Mari served the last two bowls of stew.

"Yes," the woman Morris said, "or maybe the Magistrate can tell us what really happened to those three girls, and that'll save us some time."

"I think we can persuade him," Bierce said darkly.

Mari glanced at the holstered gun at Bierce's waist, and scuttled away. Oh, no. The Magistrate would tell the Shifters everything for sure if they threatened him with a gun--and even if he didn't, Randall and Lauren would still be in danger tomorrow with the Shifters' new search strategy. She had to escape and warn Randall and Lauren, then hide with them somewhere. She hoped Randall had retrieved Stefanie from the farm with the watchdogs by this time.

That would leave only Tony to rescue. Somehow. Their chances of trying that would be the best from now until mid-tomorrow, when there'd be only one Shifter at the Fortress.

In the kitchen, Lynia entered with a tub filled with clean linens. "All dry," she said to Penna. "I'm off to hoe the garden unless there's something else you'd

126

rather I do."

Penna waved her out. "Go. You're doin' grand, miss. A fine, hard worker." She threw Mari a benevolent glance as Lynia exited. "And you, miss, are doin' much better than yesterday."

Mari smiled. "Thanks." It wasn't much of a praise, but it was praise, just the same.

The Innkeeper strode in. "Stop clucking like a pair of hens and get some work done," he growled. "You, girl, get your shoes on before you lose your dinner privileges."

Mari nodded, ignoring the sting of his words, and busied herself by sloshing lukewarm dishwater over some mugs and bowls. The Innkeeper left the kitchen. No invisible punches hit her, to her profound relief. After a while she dried her hands and peeked out to see if the Shifters needed anything more. Their table stood empty. She walked over and saw, through the Inn's front window, four cloaks flapping like monstrous raven wings as the Shifters rode away in a haze of tawny dust.

Anxiety washed over her. The Shifters had left, but the impending danger had increased. Time was running out. Hurriedly, she cleared the Shifters' table. She checked her jaw in the mirror, and saw that her bruise still looked purple, but faded. No new bruises showed. Good. The key seemed to be not letting let the Innkeeper's words--or rather, her *father's* words--affect her.

Her invisible shackles might be gone. Like Lynia, she had to make her break from years of abuse.

She dumped the dirty dishes on the counter and slipped into her shoes and socks. Time to try the escaping slave routine again. She eyed the Innkeeper, who talked with a group of ale-drinking guests in the hall, and glanced at Penna's wide back. Without further delay, she zipped through the kitchen and shot out the back door. She waved at Lynia, who looked up from where she hoed the garden. Lynia smiled and went back to hoeing.

Mari ran like crazy across the yard, slowing as she reached the area she'd fallen before, not eager to get her feet yanked out from under her again. Nothing seemed to snag at her ankles this time, however. The shackles had vanished. She'd discovered the key to her freedom.

Mari kept running, past buildings and cottages, whipping around wagons and carts and townspeople like a peasant-dressed marble in a medieval pinball machine. When she'd put a little distance between her and the Inn, she slowed. It wouldn't be good to have townspeople remember her racing by, if the Shifters questioned them later today.

A hay wagon stood parked at the edge of the golden road, the driver conversing with a pretty woman. As Mari grew closer, the man pointed down the road and said something to the woman about Lisden, and returning in three days.

Aha. A hay wagon. The standard, cliché way of escaping in the movies. She checked to see if anyone was watching, then dived into the back of the wagon, burrowing deep into the scratchy hay. Her lungs gulped in the weedy, sharp smell of the hay, the force of her heartbeat shaking her body. Would it work?

If it did, she'd get a free ride to Lisden. Almost too perfect to be true.

In a few minutes, the wagon lurched into motion. The wheels first protested with a grinding squeak, and settled into a quieter, rhythmic creaking. Through the slats of the wagon sides, Mari watched cottages and townspeople and goats file by. She nudged the hay to clear a wider breathing space by her face. The driver whistled a jaunty tune, while the sights and sounds of Permandy began to fade, replaced by trees, hills, and country quietness.

The driver ceased his whistling after a song or two. The rocking movement of the wagon lulled Mari into drowsiness. She hadn't slept well on the hard pallet the night before, with her musty blanket and the erratic, papery scuttling of cockroaches out in full force. Her eyes closed. Her mind slipped away into delightful dreams of pizza, her own bed, and indoor plumbing.

A strident, squawking chicken jolted Mari out of her sleep. A child shrieked and laughed, and a woman called out. Other voices clamored. After a short while the wagon shuddered to a creaking halt, and Mari waited until the driver had dismounted with a bounce. She heard him talking to someone. Then, after a few minutes, she couldn't hear him anymore.

Ah, good time to exit the scratchy hay. She thrashed out of her hiding place, scattering hay as she emerged. When she jumped onto the road, she saw the driver standing and glowering a few feet away, his arms folded.

"Uh, sorry," she said, straightening her skirt to cover her jeans. "I needed a ride to Lisden."

The man waved his arm in disgust. "Get outta here, you freeloader! Next time ask permission before you hitch a ride with someone."

"Sorry," Mari repeated, and crossed the road, brushing hay from her clothes. The wagon had stopped in a marketplace similar to Permandy's. She stepped over to a rickety table where a woman with a fat-cheeked baby sold squash and cabbage.

"Hi," she said. "Do you know where a boy named Kale lives with his aunt?"

"Naw, sorry," the woman said, jiggling the baby on her hip.

Mari stopped to ask four more people, with no luck. She scratched her head in puzzlement and checked the position of the sun. About halfway down the sky, late afternoon already. What rotten luck. Why didn't people know who Kale was? Surely in a small village everyone noticed when someone new came to live there. She assumed he'd originated from Permandy. Too bad she didn't know Kale's aunt's name.

She walked to the outskirts of town and spotted an elderly woman throwing grain to some geese. "Hi!" she called. "Do you know a boy who came to live with his aunt a few days ago? His name's Kale."

The old woman paused her grain-scattering to think, causing a raucous, honking protest from the geese. "No, young lady," she said after a moment, "there's no young man by that name in this village. I'm sure of it."

Mari blew out an exasperated breath. "I don't get it. Kale told me he was leaving to live with his aunt in Lisden, but I can't find anyone who knows him, or where his aunt lives."

"Lisden?" the old woman cackled. "No wonder you can't find him or his aunt. This here's Tollevale. Lisden is yonder a ways, north." She pointed down the road.

Groaning, Mari rolled her eyes. "Oh, for Pete's sake. I can't believe it."

The old woman cackled again and resumed her geese feeding.

Mari began hiking toward Lisden, feeling the indicator on her internal nuclear reactor rise to a dangerously irritated level. Dang it all. She'd napped too long in the wagon and ridden too far. She didn't have time to waste like this. The Shifters probably wouldn't reach Lisden until mid-tomorrow, but she didn't want to cut it that close.

Besides that, she had to find Kale's cottage before dark, or she'd risk another chilling encounter with an Executioner. For all she knew there might be other groups of Shifters lurking in this landscape, too. Not a happy thought. Especially walking down a main road with obviously newcomer shoes. No one around here wore rubber-soled, burgundy suede shoes with rounded laces. She might as well have a sign on her back that read "Mainworlder."

By the time she began to see scattered cottages that she hoped indicated the southern outskirts of Lisden, her stomach growled noisy complaints. She hadn't had time to nab a quick lunch before she'd left the Inn, and breakfast had only been a small bowl of gummy porridge with goat's milk. She hiked into the village. The marketplace bustled with end-of-the-day transactions, and some of the townspeople had packed up their goods already.

Mari stopped at a table where a young woman displayed woolen thread, stockings, and sweaters. "Hi," she said. "Do you know a boy named Kale, who lives with his aunt?"

The woman nodded. "Kale and his aunt live not far from me. Turn right directly after that wee old woman selling beets and turnips, and follow the path nearly to the creek. His aunt has the cottage with the two black goats."

"Thank you!" Mari said. About time she made some progress here.

She hurried along, and soon saw a cottage with two black goats. She also saw Kale standing outside, watering a row of cabbages. He looked up as she approached. His watering can thumped to the ground, sloshing water, and he ran over. "Come inside, Mari," said, shooting furtive looks up and down the road.

Mari followed Kale into the shabby but tidy cottage, which was hung with iron pots and bunches of drying herbs. A woman knelt, stirring sizzling food over the fire.

"Mari, this is my aunt," Kale said in a quick introduction. "I have a lot to tell you. Randall and Lauren left earlier this afternoon."

"What?" Mari cried. "Where are they?"

Kale's aunt stood. "You may eat with us if you'd like, while Kale tells you what's been happening."

"Thanks, I'm starved," Mari said, feeling lightheaded with worry as well as from the savory smells that filled the cottage.

They gathered dishes and food, and began to eat. "Well?" Mari prodded Kale.

"First," Kale said, "Randall tried to rescue Stef by borrowing a neighbor's wagon and pretending to be from the workhouse. He made up a story about how he was revoking her, and how he'd send a substitute later that day. But that old maniac woman with the dogs chased him off again. So Randall had to give up on Stef. To find out what happened to you, he and Lauren planned to go to Permandy this morning. I told them no, that I'd go."

"You shouldn't be seen in Permandy either," Mari said. "Someone from the mines might recognize you."

Kale's aunt flicked a firm glance from Mari to Kale. "Yes, that's what I told him. They know he's an orphan, and he could've gotten caught again."

Kale shrugged. "I wore a hood to cover most of my face. Anyway, I nosed around this morning. Found out you'd left the Haven and escaped the Inn. Didn't hear anything else until I ran into a panicked bunch of folk who'd seen four Shifters at the Magistrate's building.

The Shifters had accused the Magistrate of lying about you newcomers. Quite a big commotion."

Nodding, Mari buttered some bread. "Did the Magistrate tell the Shifters where he really sent us?"

"Yes." Kale's expression grew more sober. "But the Shifters killed him anyway, with their exploding weapons."

"What?" Mari's bread and butter suddenly lost its appeal. Her stomach knotted. "He told the truth and they still shot him?"

"Yes, because he'd lied to them. Now they're searching Permandy for all four of you."

Kale's aunt made a disparaging noise. "They won't get much cooperation from folk now. Killing a Magistrate is a serious thing indeed."

"Unless people are afraid they'll get shot too," Mari said. She drew in a shaky breath. "The Shifters will run into dead-ends when they get to Isolation and the Inn, but Stefanie will be in big trouble once the workhouse tells them she's at that farm north of here."

"Yes," Kale said. "Randall got panicked about that. He wanted to poison the farm dogs or something, to help her escape. We managed to convince him it was wiser to go into hiding right now, and not take chances while the Shifters were searching."

Mari frowned. "Where'd Randall and Lauren go?"

"They took food and water, and went to some cave near Golmer. They said you'd know where it was. I showed them a back trail to take, that ends on the hill north of Permandy."

Ah. The cave with the Portal mark. Probably a safe place. But with that plan, Stefanie would get captured by the Shifters, and Tony would remain at the Fortress. Not good. Mari nibbled her bread, not really tasting it.

"I wish I knew where the Fortress is," she said, thinking

aloud, "since only one Shifter is there right now."

"The Fortress is on the south edge of Lisden," said Kale's aunt. "But don't try to rescue your friend from there. It's too dangerous."

"Especially by yourself," Kale added. "Randall still has that master key you swiped. Maybe wait a few days. The three of you could think of a plan using the key to rescue both Tony and Stefanie from the Fortress."

Mari frowned. No, that key probably wouldn't fit anything the Shifters had. The best plan would be last-chance rescues tomorrow morning. By herself. Mari's heart knocked against her ribs at the very thought of trying to rescue Stefanie from the watchdog-infested farm, let alone trying to spring Tony from the Fortress.

But she didn't see any way around it. She had to try.

Chapter 13

Outside, in the warm evening breeze, Mari waved to Kale and his aunt, and hiked along the trail through the long fieldgrass. The sun looked about two hours away from sinking into the hills. This trail that ran behind the Lisden graveyard would take her north, but she had no intention of following it much further. She hadn't wanted to argue with Kale and his aunt, though. They probably could've talked her out of her insane rescue delusions very easily.

She swung a small knapsack that Kale's aunt had tied together for her, which held her own shoes and socks, along with goat cheese, a chunk of bread, and some sausage. She wore a pair of tattered leather shoes Kale's aunt had insisted she use. Their plan for her involved following this trail until it grew dark, ending somewhere out in the countryside north of Permandy where the curfew wouldn't be enforced. She could've slept in the fields. In the morning, she would have followed the golden road that skirted the Fraghdom Forest, and continued on to the cave.

A bird shrilled overhead, making her flinch. She looked back through the trees and brush, and saw the tiny figures of Kale and his aunt bustling around their cottage. In reality, Mari's plans were quite different. There was no way she would risk breaking curfew and sleeping in the fields anywhere, ever again. Instead, she'd stay at Sanjen's cottage tonight, even though it lay at the opposite end of Lisden. In the morning, she'd try to help Stefanie escape. If that worked, she'd stash Stefanie someplace safe or send her along the trail to the cave, while Mari hoofed it to the Fortress and scoped out Tony's situation.

But on second thought, the fifth Shifter who

guarded Tony might have a gun. And Tony would be in a locked cell or dungeon. Maybe it would be better to nab Stefanie and head straight for the cave. Like Kale had said, Randall and Lauren might have some good ideas about how to rescue Tony. Trying to rescue Stefanie would be risky enough.

Mari left the trail, looping back onto the main road and heading south through town. Her emotions tingled with anticipation. She'd love to see Sanjen again, but she didn't know if he'd be there. He'd said he traveled a lot. Did he trade goods of some sort between Lisden and Permandy? Or with Golmer in the north or Tollevale farther south? She didn't know, but she'd better think of a good excuse for her own traveling. If he felt loyal to his Shifter uncle, she didn't want to arouse his suspicions. Maybe she could say something about Randall, since she'd said her brother lived in Lisden.

She could truthfully say she'd come to see her brother, only to find out her brother had left Lisden.

The fork in the road lay south of the village. She'd seen it walking from Tollevale, with the narrow, packed dirt road branching off from the golden road, disappearing over a hill and through the trees into a less populated area of Lisden. She took the fork, and didn't walk long before she saw a cottage sitting back from the roadside. Its closed-shuttered windows and smokeless chimney made it look cold and forgotten. Her hopes sank like a two-ton stone. It didn't look like he was home.

She stepped up and knocked on the door. No one answered. She sighed, glancing around. A low wooden fence bordered the side yard, but no goats or chickens roamed outside. A rectangle of dirt and weeds lay beyond the fence, perhaps the remnants of an old garden. No other cottages stood nearby. This was the first cottage, however, so it had to be Sanjen's. The dirt road continued beyond the cottage, and over the tops of the trees she could see--

She squinted. What in this freaking dimension was *that* shape? A pointed, rough area of gray poked up through the distant trees, looking like the stone tip of a huge triangle or a pyramid. Her muscles tensed and her blood slowed into chilled stillness as she realized what she must be looking at.

The Fortress. Kale's aunt had said it lay at the south edge of Lisden. It made total sense that it would be shaped like a huge triangle.

"Whoa," she muttered. "That is way, way too close for comfort." Maybe she should've followed that trail north to the cave after all. She rapped on the door again, suddenly feeling a panicked urge to get inside, away from the sight of the Fortress, as though it possessed physical eyes to see her standing there. No one answered her knock again, so she tried the knob and found the door unlocked.

She entered, closing the door behind her. The one-roomed cottage looked dim and clean, almost stripped bare of everyday clutter. Only necessities furnished it, with a simple wooden bed and a table on one side of the room, and a sheepskin thrown in front of the fireplace. Also, a sizeable stack of split wood and a coil of rope. A few pans hanging in a row from the ceiling, with a few sacks holding grain or potatoes slumped along one wall. A small box sat on the table. The room smelled of woodsmoke and candle wax.

Definitely a man's house, but not a slob's house.

She lit a lantern, set it on the table, and strolled around, trying to imagine Sanjen living here…seeing his lean, panther-like body crossing the room, or scrubbing potatoes. Sleeping on that bed, cooking and eating his meals. She leaned over the fireplace. Ashes and a few half-burned logs of wood remained. It seemed he'd been here recently.

And she'd missed him. Bummer.

Yawning, she set down her knapsack. She curled up on the soft thick wool of the sheepskin by the fireplace, and closed her eyes. Morning would come soon. Then she would rescue Stefanie.

Somehow....

A metallic rattle and a rush of cool air penetrated Mari's sea of sleep. Her eyes opened against the foggy waves sloshing over her mind. Where was she? A door had swung ajar across the room from where she lay, and she heard a horse snorting outside. A tall figure entered and closed the door, swinging a large cloak onto a peg on the wall. By the dim light of the lantern's candle, she saw the figure turn and stop in mid-motion, catching sight of her.

Mari blinked sleep away, scrambling into a sitting position. Oh yes, she'd fallen asleep in Sanjen's cottage. Was that him? She looked closer at the man by the door. Exotic, well-toned, and incredibly hot. Yes, it was Sanjen. He stared at her, his dark-lashed eyes wide and startled for an instant before recognition erased his surprise. Then he smiled. Not a stiff half-smile as once before, but a true, brilliant smile that transformed his face. A smile of incredulous delight.

"Mari!" he said, in motion again, walking toward her. "I really didn't expect you to come here."

"Neither did I." Mari broke into a wide smile too, feeling almost giddy from his reaction. "I came to Lisden to see my brother, but he's not here anymore."

Sanjen knelt beside her, the lantern glow glinting on his earring. He touched her shoulder lightly, as if to verify she was real. "How long have you been here?"

"Not long. I dozed for a bit."

"Well, I'm glad I came home. I took my chances, since it's nearly dark out there."

"Oh, scary," Mari said with a shudder. She didn't like to think of the possibility of Sanjen being hunted by the axe-wielding Executioner.

"Are you hungry?" he asked, straightening to a stand. His face looked eager, boyish. "I've already eaten, but I could make you something."

"No thanks. I ate dinner." Mari also stood, straightening her skirt to hide her jeans.

Sanjen nodded. "All right. I'm going to make some tea, though. Would you like some?"

"Sure," Mari said. She watched him fill a metal pot with water from a barrel in one corner, then begin to light a fire. He wore boots, dark trousers, and a pirate-like tunic shirt, which not only looked awesome, but it suited him much better than a brown monk's robe.

"Got any mugs?" Mari asked.

"Sure, under that linen on the table." He chuckled. "Keeps the dust off. The tea is in the small bin by the potatoes."

They worked together in a comfortable rhythm, making preparations, adjusting to each other's movements as they had when dancing at the Haven. After that, they sat at the table, while the rich smells of mint tea and honey flowed around them. The crackling of the fire peppered the air.

Sanjen's hand slid across the table. His fingers curled around hers, and his eyes searched her face. "How long are you able to stay?"

Mari looked down at her tea, feeling melted by his direct gaze and his touch. "Only for tonight. I'm heading back toward Permandy tomorrow morning."

The snap and rustle of the fire filled the silence that met her response.

"I'm sorry to hear that," Sanjen said at last. "But then, I suppose tomorrow I have other duties I must attend to, myself."

Mari closed her eyes. She wished she could stretch out time for this evening, and speed it up tomorrow when she attempted to rescue Stefanie--and possibly got stuck walking all the way back to the cave with her. She loved being connected to Sanjen's hand. The strong, smooth, and warm sensation of his fingers twined with hers. If she ever managed to ditch this dimension, she'd have to leave him behind.

A sharp ache hit her, mid-chest. How terrible. He seemed perfect for her. She'd love to take him back to the real world and keep him. To save him from having to live here in her nightmare world. But if he traveled through the Portal with her, she'd lose her ability to dream. It was a frightening thought, to have part of her mind wiped out.

Her eyes opened to find Sanjen studying her. He gave a slight smile. "What are you thinking?"

She sipped her tea to collect her thoughts into words she could actually say. "Uh, mostly sitting here enjoying holding your hand, and wishing I could stay longer." She smiled, then felt a little appalled. Oh wow, her mother would have a major coronary if she could see her now. Sitting alone in some guy's cottage drinking tea, after only meeting him briefly two times. Someone who was four years older, and with whom she actually planned to spend the night--although she was sure she'd be sleeping on the sheepskin while Sanjen slept on his bed.

Not proper or wise, her mother would lecture, and for all Mari knew, Sanjen could be a serial killer.

140

Hmph. Her mother, always fussing and exaggerating. Man, how totally out-of-her-mind worried her mother must be about her and Randall by this time. After juggling waitressing and finances and a broken heart for the last five months, now her children had disappeared.

They had to get back. Soon.

Sanjen gave her hand a soft squeeze. "Maybe we can plan to meet again, sometime."

"Maybe," Mari said. Though she doubted it. Unless she could swing by to see him when she came back with Randall and Lauren to rescue Tony. In an ideal, best case scenario, she'd heroically scoop up Stefanie, break Tony free from the Fortress, and head to the cave, bringing Sanjen back to the real world with her. And miraculously, she wouldn't lose her ability to dream.

Right. Reality check, Mari Leigh Stratton.

Releasing her hand, Sanjen stood. He went to the fire and reached for more wood.

Mari got up and rinsed their mugs. She came back to the table, wiped the mugs with the linen, and tossed the linen over the tops. The small wooden box on the table caught her attention, so she lifted its lid and peeked in. A pair of what looked like ear buds lay inside, along with a slender metal rectangle about four inches long. Two thin cases lay next to the rectangle. Frowning, she reached in and drew out one of the thin cases. She stared. Her heart went into instant acceleration, her breathing becoming so rapid she felt hyperventilated.

The case was square and plastic, printed with a photo of a punk band called *Gnu Shoes*.

It was a CD.

She reeled away from the table, her gaze glued to the plastic square she held. No way. Two CDs in the box, along with a set of ear-bud headphones and a slender music download device. How had Sanjen gotten such modern objects? There was nothing like this in Permandy or Lisden or this entire landscape. Had his uncle given it to him? That had to be the answer, though a scary one. Only a Shifter could have traveled to a different landscape and obtained such things.

Her eyes focused on Sanjen's taut, muscular back as he added wood and poked at the fire. Then, against her will, her eyes slid to the cloak he'd thrown onto the peg by the door when he'd first come in. A jet-black cloak. Long, and full. Her legs felt leaden and stiff as she walked with the CD toward the door and halted. Her shaking hand folded back the top edge of the cloak, and she saw what she'd been afraid she'd see. A gold triangle gleamed against the black fabric.

Sanjen's outergarment wasn't a normal cloak. It was a Shifter's cloak.

Chapter 14

Mari whirled from the cloak, the sight of the triangle obliterating everything from the past few days with the force of a nuclear bomb.

No! Sanjen--a Shifter. Most likely, he was the fifth Shifter who'd stayed behind to guard Tony at the nearby Fortress.

Sanjen turned from the fire. He saw her face, and his gaze dropped to the CD in her hand. He froze. The expression on his face grew guarded, and in an instant, the atmosphere in the room spiraled and tightened.

"You're...a Shifter." She said it as a statement, not a question.

A weary look replaced Sanjen's wariness. "Does it matter?"

Mari stared at him in disbelief. Did it matter? Of course it mattered. But not in a way or to a degree he knew about. She walked a very shaky tightrope here. "Well," she said. "Every time I've seen or heard about Shifters, they're doing something terrible to someone. You mean to say you haven't done any of that? Did you make up all that stuff about your uncle being a Shifter, to pretend why you knew so much about Mainworlders and landscapes?"

Pressing his palms together, Sanjen hissed out a long breath. "No, all that I told you is true. My uncle became a Shifter when I was eight. He told me many things about their beliefs. It wasn't until I was fifteen, however, that I became old enough to join their ranks. As far as doing terrible things, well, sometimes the cause is bigger than the actions leading up to it. As Shifters we are driven to find Mainworlders. Besides, no one in any landscape suffers negative consequences if he or she cooperates."

Mari tilted her head. "So you think your cause justifies what you do--threatening people, shooting them, and burning their cottages?" She stopped, fearing she'd said too much, and flicked a glance at the closed shutters. Careful. She was trapped in this cottage for the night since darkness had fallen and Lisden's Executioner would stalk the village until dawn.

"You don't understand," Sanjen said, his words hard. "We spend our life searching for Mainworlders. The new ones arrive only once a year when the Portal gates open, and many of us die without ever having *seen* a Mainworlder. Their mental landscapes hold us prisoner. We are forced to live their nightmares, forced to wallow in their insecurities and fears. We are fighting for a better life. It's war."

"You weren't born in this landscape, were you?"

"No." The chair by the table creaked as Sanjen sat down. His voice was ragged when he spoke again, as if he struggled to control his emotions. "Mari, can't you forget a lifetime of prejudice? You've seen Shifters, but you don't really know them. We're people too. Believe me, some Shifters are more ruthless in their searching than others. For example, Bierce is my group's High Shifter. Being on the verge of Portal possibility for over twenty-five years has given him a highly aggressive edge."

"A High Shifter," she echoed. "Is that like the leader?"

"Yes. Bierce commands us, and also directs the landscape jumps. He watches for activated Portals in our region, and we try to transport there before other Shifters do."

"Why? Can't more than one group of Shifters be on a landscape at a time?"

"Not unless the first group invites them. We don't

need to invite anyone this time, since there are five of us, and five in the latest bunch of Mainworlders. Perfect."

Aha. Helpful information. This landscape held only five Shifters.

Trying to keep her breathing and steps normal, Mari walked to the table. She put the CD back in the box. "I'm really sorry I got nosy and looked in here," she said. Truly, she was. She'd revealed a snarl of hideous things she didn't want to know about, kinda like opening Pandora's box.

Sanjen gave a noncommittal grunt.

She drifted away to stand by the fire. The flames danced in angry red-orange tongues as they consumed the wood. "You must really hate the Mainworlder who built this landscape," she said, her heart feeling heavy. "The Builder of every landscape, really."

"Yes, I hate them," Sanjen said. His voice sounded as bitter as his words.

They remained silent for a few minutes, with only the crackling and snapping of the fire filling the room. Mari blinked watery eyes. He didn't know it, but he hated her. Hated her landscape, hated her nightmares, hated who she really was.

But she didn't like who he really was, either. He'd been there at the burning of Pod's cottage, had helped torch the frail old man's home. Who knew what other horrid things he'd done. Had he ever shot anyone? She looked at his profile as he stared across the room. He didn't seem to have his gun with him, but maybe he'd left it at the Fortress.

If only she could leave now, and travel at night. Tony might be alone at the Fortress with no one guarding him. Too bad she wasn't ruthless herself. In the morning while Sanjen slept, she could knock him unconscious with something hard, tie him up with that coil of rope by the firewood, and ride his horse to the Fortress. She could free Tony and head to the farm to get Stefanie. If she took Sanjen's cloak and his gun, she or Tony could masquerade as a Shifter. Releasing Stefanie would be a cinch, then.

She felt her eyes widen. Wow. That sounded like a darned good plan.

Could she really hit Sanjen, and hit him hard enough to knock him unconscious? She scanned his dark feathery hair and strong profile, and cringed. Too cruel, to think of hitting that gorgeous head. She didn't even like swatting a fly with a fly swatter. Her gaze slid to the rest of his body, to the underlying strength of his panther-like build. She shuddered. Risky. Very risky. He looked like he could move swiftly, and defend himself easily.

Shifting in his chair, Sanjen looked at her. "That case you found, it plays great music. Like magic. You might like it." His voice sounded a little forlorn.

Mari gave a wry smile. "Yes, I might." A wave of pity hit her. He lived a sad life, with his constant searching for people from another dimension, trying to find a way to escape the nightmares of Mainworlders.

"I suppose we should get some sleep," Sanjen said with a sigh. "You can sleep on the bed, and I'll sleep by the fire. I don't have another woolen, but it doesn't get that cold at night, especially by the fire."

"Oh, okay. Thanks."

Sanjen stood up and blew out the lantern candle. The glow from the fire flickered over the room, causing shadows to hover and leap on the walls like writhing demons. "Sleep well, Mari," he said, standing next to her but gazing at the floor. "Don't think about the Shifter issue too much. I'm still glad you stopped by."

She nodded, words sticking in her throat. Cripes. Hopefully her jeans wouldn't accidentally show as she slept. She cleared her throat. "Good night, Sanjen," she managed to say, looking at the soft thickness of his hair and making an unreasonable wish to touch it. "I hope you sleep well too. Try to have nice dreams."

His eyes jerked up to meet hers. "*What?*"

Mari frowned. Did he think she was making light of his situation, or how he felt? "I'm sorry," she said quickly. "I just meant I hoped you wouldn't have weird or bad dreams. Sometimes that happens to me if I'm upset about something when I fall asleep."

Sanjen's face changed from forlorn to forceful with frightening speed. He closed the distance between them in a single step and shoved her a few feet to the wall, pinning her across the neck with one strong arm and pushing up her right sleeve with the other. His breath hissed inward as he saw the Portal mark.

"You're a *Mainworlder*," he spat.

She struggled against the weight of his body wedging her against the wall. "How--what makes you think that?" she gasped. The pressure of his arm on her neck made her cough.

Sanjen held her firm. "Here, Mari, no one has dreams when they sleep. Only Mainworlders have night-time dreams." He swung her away from the wall and dragged her, stumbling, over to the stack of firewood. While keeping one hand clamped around her arm, he forced her to her knees and grabbed the rope lying on the floor.

She winced at the digging pressure of his fingers. Tears pricked her eyes. "Sanjen, stop! You're hurting me."

"I need to make sure you don't escape." He knotted the rope around her wrists, cinching her hands together

147

behind her back, then yanked her over and shoved her onto the sheepskin to tie her ankles. He made an angry exclamation when the skirt bunched and showed her jeans. "I must be getting lax, or stupid," he muttered. "A Mainworlder right in front of me, and I can't tell the difference between you and a confounded villager."

"I'm still the same person," Mari said. "You asked me to be open-minded about you being a Shifter, and now--"

"That's very different," Sanjen snapped. "Your kind has made my life miserable from the day I was born. I've seen landscapes with daily hurricanes and dissolving cities, landscapes with werewolves and vampires and writhing hordes of rabid animals. Don't tell me it doesn't make a difference. I'll be glad to transport through the Portal with you and your friends, because that means five fewer landscapes will exist here in this dimension. And I'll be especially delighted to wipe out your foul, dreaming mind." He tugged the rope tight, making her yip in pain.

She glared at him as he stood to hover above her. Dang, and to think she'd been reluctant about bashing his head with something hard to knock him out. He certainly didn't have any qualms about hurting her.

Sanjen folded his arms. "So the Magistrate lied about Ranser. You got sent to the Haven instead. Why?"

"I had a spider bite," Mari said in a near-whisper. "Why were you there at the Haven?"

"I hate the Permandy Inn, even more than I hate staying at this landscape's Fortress," Sanjen said.

Mari watched him warily. It must have been Sanjen she'd seen with the other Shifter in the slime rain. They hadn't left Permandy early as the other Shifter had suggested, and Sanjen must've gone to the Haven for the night rather than staying at the Inn.

"Where are the other two girls?" Sanjen demanded.

"I don't know. I went to the Haven, and the Magistrate sent them somewhere else."

Sanjen's eyes glittered in the leaping firelight. "And the boy who escaped the mines? Is he your brother, or was that a feeble excuse to explain why you came to Lisden?"

"He's my brother," Mari said. "He left Lisden, and I don't know where he is now."

"Where's your Portal?"

Mari shook her head. "I'd be an idiot to tell you that."

"If you're smart, you'll tell me everything you know," Sanjen said, his voice steely. "But no worries. As it happens, your friend Tony has already told us the Portal is in a cave north of Permandy. I was seeing if you'd tell me the truth."

"Did you torture him to get him to say that?" Mari asked, her heart pounding.

"What do you think?" Sanjen said. Then he swore. "Good thing I caught you to redeem myself," he growled, "since I ignorantly told you at the Haven how to activate the Portal."

Mari frowned. "If you already know where the Portal is, why didn't one of you travel through it with Tony?"

"Impossible. Activation doesn't work unless all five of you are there."

Mari studied Sanjen, her thoughts racing. So the Shifters wouldn't go to the cave for Portal activation until they'd captured all five of them. Randall and Lauren would be safe for now--unless the Shifters guessed the cave served as a rendezvous place.

"Get some sleep," Sanjen said, and turned on his

heel to go to his bed.

Mari listened to the fire crackle for a long while. She cried a torrent of silent, frustrated tears. What a fool she was, to have come here instead of sleeping in the fields and continuing on to the cave. Now she was captured and tomorrow Stefanie would likely be discovered, making a total of three of them in the Shifters' clutches.

This was her second lame mistake, and both mistakes had involved wanting to see Sanjen again. She'd read way too many romance novels. The plucky heroine, against all odds, longing to be with the handsome guy she'd fallen in love with at first sight. Struggling against the circumstances that kept them apart, overcoming those obstacles, and living forever in true bliss. Bah. Like her relationship with Brad, her connection with Sanjen had been formed from wispy and insubstantial clouds of romantic dreams.

She wouldn't have guessed in a gazillion years that Sanjen was a Shifter, and able to turn on her in one intense, frightening moment.

She fell into a fitful sleep, and slept hard. The next thing she knew, she heard clunking and shifting in the room. She groaned. Ugh, her whole body felt stiff. The tight ropes had rubbed on her wrists, and even with the protection of her socks, her ankles felt sore. Sanjen swept across her view, wearing his black Shifter cloak. She shuddered.

The transformation from gentle Haven dancer into a cruel and dangerous Shifter was complete.

Sanjen knelt at her feet and began untying the ropes around her ankles. "This is only so you can walk to the Fortress," he warned. "Don't get any ideas about running away."

Mari glared. "My, aren't we friendly this morning."

150

With a tight-lipped smile, Sanjen stood and motioned for her to stand up. He steadied her by her arm as she lurched into an awkward stand. After she'd gotten her balance, he propelled her to the table and pushed her into a chair.

"What's this?" he said, grabbing her knapsack and carrying it to the table.

"My stuff," Mari said. "Leave it alone."

It was Sanjen's turn to glare. He opened the knapsack and grunted when he saw the shoes and socks. The cheese, bread, and sausage he placed on the table. "Take a bite," he said, holding the bread out to her.

"If you'd untie me, I could eat that by myself," she said. "It'd be a lot easier and faster."

His eyes flicked over her face and down her arms. "You're hardly in a position to tell me what to do right now. You're lucky I'm feeding you at all." After a brief pause, however, he untied one of her hands and tied the loose end to the chair. He divided the food, and they ate without speaking or looking at each other. The air between them sizzled with tension.

"Put your own shoes on," he ordered when they'd finished eating, "and take off that peasant skirt--it doesn't suit who you really are. I'm going to get my horse ready."

One-handed, Mari fumbled with her socks and shoes while he strode across the room and out the door. The faint rays of daylight streaked the room as the door opened. The horse snorted outside. She wriggled out of her skirt and kicked it into the corner. Because of the ropes, she didn't try to take off the peasant blouse. Sanjen returned, and she grimaced as he untied her from thc chair and hauled her by the arm across the room. Outside, he held one end of the rope and mounted his horse.

"Now, you will start walking," Sanjen said, kicking his horse into motion.

Feeling like a dog on a leash, Mari walked. She studied the length of rope between her wrist and Sanjen's hand as he rode. How firmly was he holding that rope end? If she tugged when he least expected it, could she race off down the road? Or, better yet, if she dashed toward the bushes, maybe she could run where the horse couldn't follow her. Sanjen would still chase her on foot, but she had a better chance of losing him that way.

Or not. She sighed. "You know," she said up to Sanjen, "I had no idea I was building this landscape. I didn't mean to. I didn't even know this dimension existed."

Sanjen twisted around so fast she flinched. "You're the *Builder*?" he said, looking back at her with an expression of wild shock.

"Uh, yeah," Mari said. She fell silent as his shocked expression turned to disgust.

"Helpful to know," he retorted, turning to face forward again.

"Why?" Mari asked.

He didn't answer.

She began bunching the rope into her hand. "Why, Sanjen?" she asked again, making no attempt to hide the worry and fear in her voice. "What difference does it make?"

"You'll see," was all he said.

"I shouldn't have said anything," she muttered. She scanned the trees and bushes on both sides of the road, and saw that the left side featured a thick tangle of blackberry bushes. A small break in the thicket appeared on her left. Aha. A place where Sanjen couldn't take his horse. She had to act now.

With a tremendous jerk, she yanked on the rope. The rope whipped from Sanjen's hand, and she took off running. Behind her, he yelled in rage, and the horse whinnied. She crashed through the break in the brambles and ran full speed through the woods, trailing the rope and kicking up a flurry of pine needles.

Before long, the thumps of Sanjen's feet sounded not far behind her. She could hear the rush of his labored breathing and his cloak snapping. The sounds grew closer. His fingertips brushed her shoulder, snatching at her peasant blouse.

He missed. She ran faster, panting. The trees and bushes passed by in a green blur. Sanjen's hand found her hair, tangled in it, and grabbed tight. She screamed as he slowed her into a careening halt by her hair, and his other arm snaked around her waist. They staggered together and fell onto the forest floor, hard.

Coughing in the rising powder of forest debris, Mari thrashed. Sanjen pinned her flat against the ground, his weight and strength pressing the fight out of her. She went limp, giving up. They lay still, only their chests moving, heaving and gulping in great amounts of air.

Sanjen's face, inches from hers, looked livid. "That was a very stupid thing to do," he growled.

"I had to try," she said, matching the ferocity of his expression. They glowered at each other for another few seconds. She looked at the exotic darkness of his eyes and lashes, the curve of his mouth, and all at once her anger crumbled. Blinking sudden tears, she looked away. "I don't know why I ever thought you liked me," she said brokenly.

Sanjen made a tortured noise and pulled her up with him. "Walk," he ordered.

They returned to the horse and continued on, this time with Mari riding in front of Sanjen, his left arm an unyielding band around her waist. In a few minutes they reached the Fortress, with its pyramid-shaped silhouette standing like an ill omen against the rising sun. At the entrance, Sanjen rang a bell, and a small man with long greasy hair appeared in the doorway. He wore black with a gleaming gold triangle on his shirt pocket, but no cloak.

"West, take care of the horse," Sanjen ordered, and dismounted with Mari while the man nodded and took the horse's reins.

"A message rider from Bierce arrived not long ago, sir," West informed Sanjen. "It seems the Magistrate of Permandy lied about the girls. The Magistrate has been punished accordingly, and they're doing a sweeping search of Permandy, north to south. They will arrive to search Lisden later this morning."

"Thank you, West," Sanjen said. "After the rider and his horse has rested, send word to Bierce that I've captured one of the girls."

"Yes, sir."

Mari watched the man lead the horse around the side of the building. "You know," she told Sanjen, "if you guys had cell phones, you'd find out this stuff a lot faster."

"Shut up," Sanjen growled, and led her inside.

They entered a hallway and turned left. Sanjen kept his grasp tight on her arm. With the other hand, he pulled a modern lighter from an inner cloak pocket and lit a lantern sitting on a small table. He gave her the lantern to carry, and they headed down a flight of stone steps. The air grew colder, more dank. The musty smells of dirt and mold and closed-in spaces accosted Mari's nose. She tried to breathe normally, but her heart began thumping a frenzied rhythm, jolting all calmness from her body.

How would she ever get out of this dungeon?

They came to a sturdy wooden door, and Sanjen lifted a ring of keys from a nail. He herded her inside and took the lantern from her, placing it on the floor. He unlocked the second cell in a row of four. The small cell was bare except for a chamber pot and a splintery wooden bed along the back side. As he thrust her inside and the barred door clanged behind her, a figure moved in the first cell.

"Tony!" Mari cried, a lump forming in her throat as the figure moved to the bars between them.

"Hey, Mari," Tony said, gripping the bars with tense fists. "Are you okay?"

"Cut the chatter," Sanjen said, removing the key from the cell lock as Mari untied the rope around her wrist. Mari, you will now tell me where the other three of your kind are, and what they look like."

"I--I told you," Mari said. "I don't know where anyone is."

"What does your brother look like?"

"Like a brother. Two eyes, a nose, an annoying grin. What more do you want me to say?"

"Hair color and body build?"

Mari glared. "I don't have to tell you anything. Bierce has probably already captured him anyway, if they're doing a search of Permandy."

"Ah, so he's in Permandy?"

"I don't know."

"You're not being very cooperative," Sanjen said. "I think you need some convincing to be more informative."

Tony shook and jangled the bars between the cells. "Don't you hurt her--"

"Quiet," Sanjen said. "I'm tired of asking, Mari. Describe your friends."

"No," Mari said, cringing. What would he do if she didn't tell him?

"I'll be back," Sanjen said, his voice flat and ominous. He stalked from the room. The sounds of his footsteps echoed with dull thuds as he climbed back up the stairs.

Mari rushed over to Tony. In the dim light of the lantern, he looked tousled and weary. "Tony, are you okay? Are they feeding you?"

"Yeah," Tony said with a grunt. "It isn't the Hilton, but I'm all right. They haven't done too much to me, except threaten me and knock me around a little."

"That's terrible."

"Less abuse than that mining foreman, actually. An improvement in this whole zoned-out place." He gave a crooked smile.

"Not funny." A hard lump formed and stuck in Mari's throat. "It's all my fault. I'm really sorry."

Tony reached through the bars and enfolded her hands with his. "Hey, chiquita," he said, his voice gentle and soothing, "how is it your fault? That doesn't make any sense."

"I made this dimension. It's built from my dreams and nightmares. The triangle in the cave is a Portal, and all five of us have to activate it and get back home."

Tony shrugged. "Why don't we go with the Shifters? They want to take us there."

"No!" Mari said. "If you take someone from this dimension back with you, the dreaming part of your mind is wiped out. Destroyed."

"Oh." Tony grimaced. "When the Shifters asked, I made up stuff about what you all looked like, but now I wish I hadn't told them where the Portal was. I wouldn't have, except they said they'd captured one of you girls, and I thought I heard one of you screaming."

156

Mari frowned. "Couldn't have been. I wonder if it was a recording of a girl screaming or something."

"Hmm. It did sound odd and echoey. You mean Stefanie and Lauren aren't captured?"

"No," Mari said, throwing a glance at the door and lowering her voice. "Lauren and Randall headed to the cave yesterday, and I was supposed to meet them there. Stefanie's at a farm north of Lisden--" She broke off as she heard footsteps, her hands sliding from Tony's.

The door grated and shuddered open, and Sanjen entered carrying a metal box about two feet wide. He threw a disdainful glance at Tony and stood in front of Mari's cell. "Last chance, Mari. Tell me about the other three." A slight yet horrible scraping came from the box he held.

Mari shrank against the back wall by the bed. What did Sanjen have in the box? What could she tell him that wouldn't reveal something crucial? Her voice came out thin and shaky. "W-we got separated. Tony and my brother got sent to the mines. The other two girls got sent somewhere else. To the workhouse, I think. I never saw anyone again until Tony, just now."

"You lie!" Sanjen yelled, slamming his free hand against the bars, making them rattle. "At the Haven you told me you'd had an argument with your brother. That was *after* he'd escaped the mines."

Oh. Oops. Mari squinted at Sanjen. "Okay, so I saw him. We had an argument and I went back to the Haven. He went somewhere else."

"Where was he was going?"

"He didn't say."

"You're lying again," Sanjen said, his voice tight. "And I don't appreciate it. Since you're the Builder of this cursed landscape, we've collected a very persuasive way of making you talk." His eyes flicked to the box he held. "It's your choice."

Mari stared at the box with dread. "What's in there?"

"Tell me where your brother is and what your friends look like, or you'll find out." His voice lowered to a deadly murmur. "The hard way."

"No, Sanjen. No," she whispered.

Sanjen hissed through clenched teeth and pulled the cell key from a pocket in his cloak. He unlocked her cell and pushed the box in, unlatching and flipping back the lid. "I'll return in a few minutes to hear you talk," he said, his words grim. He stalked from the room, the heavy door slamming behind him.

Mari's gaze riveted to the box. The scrabbling grew louder.

"What's in there?" Tony asked, worried.

"I don't know," Mari said, more a breath than audible words. She had a suspicion, though, and hoped she wasn't right.

The noises from the box grew louder yet. She heard the sliding and scuffling sounds of something trying to get out. Something alive. Something…multi-legged.

A wicked black point poked above the edge of the box, followed by another, then another. A hideous hairy body appeared, five inches across. Its mouth chewed the air, while a second set of legs scrabbled into view and the rustling continued, down in the box.

Spiders. Vampire spiders.

Chapter 15

Mari squeezed her fingernails deep into her palms and screamed, splitting the air with a blast of sheer volume and terror. As her scream faded and died, she pressed herself against the back wall of her cell. Her body shook, and her armpits prickled with instant sweat. The first spider clambered from the box and skittered across the floor toward her.

"Kick it!" Tony cried. "Don't let it climb on you."

With a moan, Mari looked at the grotesque, hurtling spider. Kick it? She didn't want her foot anywhere near that freaky creature. It might latch onto her foot or her jeans like it had in the Fraghdom Forest.

The spider scuttled closer--four feet away, then three, then two. With a strangled scream, Mari kicked it as hard as she could. It hurtled backward and bounced off the bars on the opposite side of the cell.

"Good job!" Tony said. "Here comes another one, soccer-mama. Get ready."

The second spider headed toward her as a third and a fourth spider crawled from the box. They scrambled across the cell floor, and one of them veered to the bars by Tony. He kicked it and sent it flying across her cell. Mari kicked another one, but it fell short, landing halfway across the cell. She kicked again, and kept kicking as the spiders flailed, righted themselves like the zombie undead, and came back at her.

There were only five of them, but they were determined. Hungry.

Three of them came toward her at once. Mari looked around the cell, shivering. Could she bash one with her chamber pot? Maybe, but she couldn't reach the pot. She started to kick at the closest spider, but the other two were too close. Oh, no. She wasn't going to make it--one of them would grab onto her for sure. With a shriek, she climbed onto the low wooden bed. Her sweat grew clammy on her skin as the spiders surrounded the bed, hovering near it but not touching it. They seemed to shudder, the juices from their heaving mouths dripping onto the floor.

She eyed their inky fat bodies with horror. "Don't crawl up here, or jump," she whispered. "Please, please don't be able to jump."

The fourth spider joined the three around her, while the fifth one scurried into Tony's cell. Tony hurled his empty metal chamber pot at it, hitting it. It halted from the impact, then staggered toward him again. "These things refuse to die!" Tony yelled. "What are they made of, rubber?"

"I don't know," Mari gasped. "I wish we could get them back into the box."

"There's an idea. Trap 'em." Tony kicked his spider away and lunged for his chamber pot again. With a bloodcurdling battle yell, he grabbed the pot and slammed it over the spider, trapping it underneath. It scrabbled with wild fury, scraping against the metal. "Got one," he crowed. "Not sure I can let go, though. They seem really strong." He sat on the top of the pot to hold it down.

Mari felt a sudden thump of pressure on her foot and looked down. To her horror, she saw that one of the spiders had jumped. She had no breath left for a scream. Frantic, she shook her foot, but the spider clutched at her jeans and held on. "Oh, no. Nononononooo," she wailed as it began climbing up her leg. She felt the points of its legs pierce her jeans as it climbed, pricking her like needles.

"Hit that thing, Mari!" Tony urged.

She moaned, clenched her teeth, and hit it. Her fist

160

made a sickening thump against its body. It wobbled but held tight. She hit it again. In a flash, the spider swiveled and latched onto her hand, wrapping its dark legs around her wrist. A sharp stab of pain flared as the spider bit into the flesh near the base of her palm. She gave a mangled, dry scream. The spider kept biting, sucking deeper into her skin.

Pain lanced her wrist and shot up her arm. She reeled back on the bed, gulping for air, growing lightheaded. Off--she had to get it *off!* She bashed her spidered arm against the wall, trying to dislodge the feeding beast, but it hung on.

Tony made an angry, helpless noise from the other cell.

Another spider jumped and landed on her shoe. Her free hand flailed, searching the bed for some kind of weapon--anything. Bits of string and wool came up in her hand. As her fingertips found a dry bit of bread, a splinter from the bed snagged her blouse sleeve. She looked down and grabbed the thick splinter, prying it off with a cracking rip.

"Gross!" she cried, in anticipation of what she was about to do. Nearly blinded by tears, she stabbed the splinter into the spider on her wrist. The spider frothed greenish blood and writhed. It fell from her arm, its pointed legs convulsing around the splinter, hitting the floor with a soft thud. Once there, it shriveled to half its size and lay motionless.

Mari gaped. Was it dead? She blinked sweat from her eyes and ripped another wood shard from the bed. She punctured the spider on her shoe and twisted out of reach as a third spider leaped for the knee of her jeans. The shoe spider convulsed and crumpled around the shard, then rolled off the bed. The third spider missed her knee and landed on the bed instead. There, it shuddered and squirmed like she'd stabbed it, but she hadn't touched it.

"They don't like wood!" Mari cried. "That's why they didn't climb onto the bed."

"You've got to be kidding," Tony said, as Mari stabbed the third spider with another piece of wood. "You mean, like real vampires?"

"Guess so." Mari armed herself with a shard and got off the bed, kicking the remaining spider a few feet away. She dashed to the metal box and slammed it over the last spider. "There," she panted, dropping the shard, "now I don't have to stab any more of those nasty things--"

Footsteps thudded on the stairs outside the heavy door.

Mari looked around, wild-eyed. An idea sprang into her mind. She put her finger to her lips in a silent signal to Tony, and threw herself down near the door of the cell with her bloodied wrist stretched out. Her hair covered most of her face, and she tried to slow her breathing. Her wrist throbbed as the heavy door to the cell area opened and footsteps clomped over to her cell. Something Sanjen carried clunked onto the floor.

"What are you trying to prove, Sanjen?" she heard Tony accuse. "Those spiders are vicious, and you set five of them on her."

Sanjen didn't answer. The key slid into the lock of Mari's cell and the door creaked open. "Did she pass out from fear?" he asked Tony. "She couldn't have lost that much blood already." Mari felt Sanjen's boot nudge her arm. She lay still as he paused. "Are those spiders *dead?*" She heard him step across the cell, and she opened her eyes into slits to see him bend to the metal box where the live spider crouched underneath. As he tipped it, she scrambled to her knees and tumbled out the cell door that Sanjen had left ajar.

Sanjen sputtered a string of swear words and backed away from the box, letting it crash down over the spider as Mari slammed the door and grabbed the key sticking out from the lock. Sanjen spun toward the door and lunged across the cell, but Mari had already backed away. She avoided his clutching hand through the bars and breathed a sigh of relief as he shook the cell door and found it locked.

"Mari, you're going to regret this," Sanjen said through gritted teeth. "We'll still find you."

"Not if I can help it," Mari said, dashing to Tony's cell and trying one of the keys in his lock. That key didn't fit, but the next one did. Tony rushed from the cell.

"West!" Sanjen bellowed. "They're escaping!"

The sound of Sanjen's yell reverberated around the dungeon, and then he broke off, cursing again. Without Tony's weight holding down the chamber pot, the spider underneath had broken free and was scurrying straight toward Sanjen. Mari and Tony slipped out the heavy door. They left Sanjen to his battle and the gruesome sight of three oozing spiders lying with their wicked legs frozen in mid-air.

Mari mounted the stone steps two at a time, with Tony close behind her. Sanjen's shouts echoed from the dungeon as she reached the top and peered around the corner, down the hallway. All clear. Somewhere, though, that greasy servant West and the message rider lurked. With Tony, she darted for the front door. They slipped outside into the glare of morning sunlight. Relieved, Mari saw no one.

"Let's get outta here," Tony whispered, moving toward the treeline.

"Wait," Mari said. "We have to get to Stefanie this

163

morning before the Shifters do, and high-tail it to the cave. Maybe we should take a horse."

Tony threw her a dubious glance. "Have you ever ridden one? I haven't."

"Uh, a little," Mari said, waving him around to the back of the Fortress. "I had a friend in California who owned horses."

They ran with stealthy feet and looked around the back edge of the Fortress. Pens with goats, pigs, chickens, and the two horses lay fifty yards away, with West walking toward the Fortress. West climbed a set of steps and disappeared into a back door.

"Go fast," Tony said. "Now he'll be able to set Sanjen free."

"Not unless they have another set of keys," Mari said, flinging the ring of keys into the bushes. She and Tony sprinted over to the horses.

"There now, easy. Good boy," Mari cooed to the message rider's horse, stroking its sides to settle its nerves after their hasty approach. She led the horse to the low fence by the pigs and motioned for Tony to use the fence to climb up.

Tony swallowed. "Okay, here goes. You riding with me?"

"Sure," Mari said, then exchanged a wary look with Sanjen's sleek, black horse. "Or maybe I should ride the other horse so they can't follow us."

"Okay, so how do I drive this thing?" Tony asked, looking a little panicked as he took the reins.

"Make a clicking noise and nudge his ribs with your heels to start going," Mari said hastily, swinging onto Sanjen's horse. "Pull back on the reins to stop. Angle right to go right, left to go left."

"Yeah, really easy," Tony muttered. "Like a motorcycle, only with legs." He followed her lead at clicking and nudging, and their rides sprang into motion.

After a few yards Mari kicked her horse into a trot, and Tony did the same, wobbling a little. As they reached the front of the Fortress, the door opened and a red-haired man barreled out. The message rider.

"They're out here!" the man yelled to someone inside. He shook his fist at Tony. "That's my horse, you bloody thief!"

Mari leaned forward and held onto the reins. Their horses sped up, hooves clopping over the dirt road, heading back toward Sanjen's cottage and past it. The blood on Mari's wrist dried in garish streaks, and her puncture marks stung. Her heart pounded like African drums in her chest and throat.

"You're doing great!" she called to Tony, who flicked her a brief, tense smile.

They skirted Lisden, paralleling but avoiding the main road in case Shifters rode there. Mari slowed and breathed more easily as she sighted the graveyard near the trail to Permandy. Now she knew where she was. She coached Tony to slow his horse into a more moderate pace.

"There's a trail back here we can follow for a while," she told Tony as they passed crumbling square markers and gravestones. "The farm where Stefanie's been taken is in between Lisden and Permandy."

"Gotcha," Tony said. "So we rescue the fair maiden from the farm, head back to the cave, and blast back into our own dimension. We cry and weep from sheer gratitude, then go home and sleep in our cozy beds. For about a week."

She smiled, a pang of yearning for home hitting her. "Hopefully just like that, yeah."

"Thanks for rescuing me, Mari, even though I'm not

165

a fair maiden."

She had to laugh at that. "No problem. I'm sure you would've done the same for me."

"Absolutely," Tony said, his voice and expression dead-serious, "and I have to say, you are one brave chiquita. Those spiders may be part of your own personal nightmares, but they are pretty scary critters for anyone to look at, let alone have to combat."

"Thanks," Mari murmured. Actually, she still felt shaky and freaked out about that spider battle. She pointed out the trail and they directed their horses toward it.

"Why you, though?" Tony asked.

"What, why is this my landscape and not someone else's?"

"Yeah, I mean, we could've been transported into a place built by my dreams and nightmares--or Stefanie's or Randall's or Lauren's."

"I have no idea," Mari said. "Bad luck I guess. But I'll sure be glad when it's all over."

"You think Sanjen will get out of that cell and come after us?"

"It'll be pretty slow going without a horse."

"Unless the other Shifters come back and get him."

"Yeah," Mari said, "and the other Shifters are supposed to arrive in Lisden later this morning. We don't have much time." The flash-frozen snapshot image of Sanjen's face sprang into her mind, distorted with rage and hatred in the cell. Sanjen would be even more furious when he discovered she'd taken his horse. She'd better pray he never caught up with her.

"I wonder if Sanjen got bitten," she said, more to herself than Tony.

Tony shrugged. "Would serve him right. I think he knew about the critters not liking wood though. He brought a stick and a wooden box with him. You probably didn't see that, lying on the floor pretending to be passed out."

"No, I didn't."

"Great plan too, by the way. Uh, how's your bite feeling?" Tony asked, looking at the streaks and splatters of blood by her palm and on her peasant blouse sleeve.

"It's throbbing. I need to wash it the first chance I get, to rinse their nasty spit off."

Tony murmured a sympathetic agreement, and they fell silent. They'd ridden for about ten minutes when Mari spotted the backside of a cottage, and an extensive garden. The cottage looked small, and she saw no dogs. Were they close to the farm yet? She chewed on her lip, squinting through the foliage of the woods as they rode. For all they knew, the farm in question could be on the other side of the golden road. It'd be awfully risky to stop at a cottage and ask for directions, but they might have to.

"Look," Tony said after another few minutes. "Think that's it?"

Mari looked where he pointed. They were nearing the backside of an old farmhouse set back from the golden road by a narrow stretch of dirt road, with rows and rows of corn waving in a field. A number of workers toiled in the cornfield and in the large garden nearby. Goats, ducks, and chickens wandered in a fenced area. Two barrel-chested dogs loped behind the house, nipping and snapping at each other.

"It's very possible that's it," Mari said. "Let's ride closer and see if we can see Stefanie."

They aimed their horses off the trail and toward the farm. As they neared the stretch of dirt and weeds that flanked the garden, Tony eased his horse into a halt.

"There she is!" he said, keeping his voice low.

Mari spotted Stefanie's white-blonde hair and curvy figure briefly by the steps, and then Stefanie went back inside. "Good. How do we get her out of there?"

"I think we should leave the horses here by these trees, and creep up on foot," Tony said. "We can scope things out better that way."

"Okay." Mari swung down, as did Tony, and they edged closer. Behind the farmhouse, one of the big dogs gave a rumbling bark. Mari looked to see it staring straight at her, even though it was over a hundred yards away. Her muscles tensed. Dang. Their dismount and approach must've been too clumsy.

"Uh-oh," Tony said.

"Yep, we're gonna have company," Mari said.

The dog shot toward her and Tony, a charcoal-black streak of fangs and ferocious noise. The other dog in the yard joined it, breaking into a riotous barking. More dogs burst into sight, coming from all sides of the house. The dogs closed the distance between them in a flash and surrounded Mari and Tony like a pack of starved wolves. Their eyes rolled back, showing rims of white. Their teeth snapped the air by Mari's hips and hands.

Mari and Tony stopped, paralyzed in their tracks.

Chapter 16

Mari pressed her palms against the thighs of her jeans, trying to avoid having any part of her sticking out for the dogs to bite. She flinched as the charcoal gray dog lunged, snapping, by her elbow. The pandemonium of barking and vicious snarls vibrated her nerves and made her feel unsteady and weak.

Tony swore. "Too late to run for the horses."

The horses, despite being a fair distance away, stamped and snorted from the noise of the dogs. A mottled gray dog with a hunk missing from one ear nipped at Tony's ankle, making him jump. He swore again.

"Hold!" a stern female voice commanded in a strident shout.

Mari looked toward the farmhouse to see a wiry woman marching across the dirt. The woman's hands clenched into bony fists, her eyes were daggers of blue. A frizz of shock-white hair stood up from her scalp like a permanent gone bad, while the skirt of her dress flapped with her movement like a conquering flag.

Ah. This must be the white-haired maniac of a woman Randall had mentioned. The pack of dogs quieted but held their ground, snarling with their lips curled back from their teeth.

"What you up to now, eh?" the old woman shrilled. "Stealin' my corn? I don't take kindly to thieves, you two youngsters."

"We're not stealing anything," Tony said. "We're from the workhouse, and--"

The woman gave a piercing screech. "Oh, no they don't! They're not pulling that on me again. I bought that gal fair and square, and I ain't fixin' to trade her. Even if she is defective." She stopped all of a sudden, focusing on Mari. "Or mebbe you're a better worker. That other gal's a lily-livered fusspot, and you look a bit sturdier even though you're small." She cackled. "Yes, mebbe we need *both* you gals, I'm thinkin'."

"No, that's not what we're here for--" Mari began.

"Get inside," the woman ordered Mari, pointing her bony hand toward the back door. "Unless you like stayin' out here with the dogs."

Mari traded a panicked look with Tony.

"Ma'am," Tony said. "This girl isn't a servant from the workhouse. She--"

The horses snorted and whinnied behind them, and the old woman's head snapped to attention. "What's that you got over there? Some fine lookin' horses, eh?" She cackled. "Reckon I'll keep those for myself. So scat now, boy. I got me plenty of male workers for the corn and the garden. I only need female servants for the house and to tend to the dogs."

The dogs growled, pacing a few feet away. Mari swallowed. She and Tony weren't going to be able to talk themselves out of this one, not with the woman commanding these blasted dogs. "Go, Tony," she said, meeting his concerned gaze while the old woman tromped over to the horses and grabbed their reins.

"I'm not abandoning you and Stefanie," Tony said. "I'll wait for you on the trail."

Wary of the dogs, Mari moved closer, speaking fast. "I can still try to escape with Stefanie. Don't wait around here, okay? It's not safe. Head for the cave and we'll join you there. If we happen to get caught, you can help Randall and Lauren free us."

Tony frowned. "I'm not leaving until I know you and Stefanie will be able to escape."

"We'll escape," Mari declared, "even if I have to poison these danged dogs like Randall wanted to do."

Tony's eyebrows raised. "Well, I suppose if anyone can escape a place, you can."

"Stefanie and I will catch up with you soon," Mari promised, sounding optimistic but not feeling it. Mostly, she wanted Tony to get to safety. "The trail ends north of Permandy. After that, follow the golden road to the cave."

"Okay, good luck," he said, and surprised her by encircling her in a brief but firm hug.

"Run fast," Mari said. "The Shifters won't be far behind once they figure out all five of us are free. They know where the cave is, and they'll know Sanjen told me how to activate the Portal."

Tony nodded, looking disgruntled.

The white-haired woman passed with the horses, whistling for the dogs. "Get off my property," she ordered Tony, then gave a curt nod at Mari. "You, missy, come with me."

Mari threw one last glance at Tony, who gave her a resigned salute and trotted away toward the trail.

"Burt!" the old woman yelled toward the garden. "Come tie these horses by the side of the house 'til I decide where to put 'em."

"Yes, ma'am," a man working in the garden answered, running over and taking the horses.

Mari accompanied the white-haired woman to the back door. The pack of dogs parted like a growling, dark sea to let her pass. She entered the house and saw a hall lined with baskets, muddy burlap sacks, and piles of vegetables.

"Rinse that blood off your wrist here," the old woman said, indicating a tub of water. She watched with her hands on hips while Mari splashed her spider bite clean. When she finished, Mari trailed after the woman again.

The kitchen lay next to the hall, worn and cluttered but thankfully cleaner and less rancid than the kitchen at the Permandy Inn. In one corner under a hanging row of dented pots and pans, Stefanie kneeled, stripping cooked meat from huge bones into a wooden tub. She wore her jeans and sweater, not peasant clothing. Dirt smudged her face and clothes, and her once-silky hair looked matted and dirty. She glanced up in surprise when Mari came in.

The white-haired woman pointed at the tub. "Start workin' here," she said to Mari. "Help this fussy gal get the dog bones ready, and add the meat to the pot so the cook can start fixin' the mid-day meal. The workers will be hungry." She marched off, her bony fists swinging.

Mari sank to her knees next to Stefanie and began picking meat off. "Hey, Stefanie."

"Hey, Mari," Stefanie acknowledged, with a slight curl to her lip. "So you got sentenced to hard labor here, too?"

Throwing a cautious glance at a potbellied man who swaggered in and began chopping onions, Mari tried not to bristle. She leaned closer. "Tony and I came to help you escape, but that maniac woman sent him away. You and I can't stay long here much longer, because I heard the Shifters say they'll be here later this morning."

"Some lame rescue," Stefanie hissed. "You're stuck here, same as I am! I can't believe it. You don't know how it's been for me, feeding those gross beasts, cleaning up after them outside while they nip and snarl at my elbows. They'd rip me to shreds in a second if that woman snapped her fingers to do it."

"We'll get out of here somehow," Mari said, her hope deflating despite her words of assurance. "Randall wanted to try to poison the dogs. Maybe we can try that."

"With what?" Stefanie scoffed. "In case you haven't noticed, there's no cyanide or arsenic or even rat poison around here. And the dogs might not die immediately, which would be really sickening."

Mari frowned. Man, this girl was all prickles and snarls. Worse than Randall, even. She almost wished she and Tony had kept going on the trail, and not stopped here. "How about bribing them with these bones?"

"There are eleven or twelve dogs, and they get bones like this every other day. They fight each other for them, even when they have their own already."

"Then we toss the bones and escape while they're fighting."

"It's not that easy, Mari. These dogs are trained to guard, and if you want to risk getting a set of wicked dog fangs in your leg, you go right ahead. But count me out." Stefanie clunked the cleaned bone she'd been working on into a pail of other bones and stood up. "Here, you finish this slimy job. I'll start chopping veggies."

Mari fumed while Stefanie crossed the kitchen and checked with the potbellied man about which vegetables were destined for the mid-day stew. Well, if they couldn't use dog bones, then what? Some of the meat? She'd bet the dogs didn't usually get meat. Keeping an eye on Stefanie and the cook, Mari stripped off her peasant blouse and rolled a good portion of meat into it. Then she slipped out of the kitchen and into the back hall, which luckily happened to be empty of anyone. She stashed her cloth-rolled burrito inside a basket, and looked around. She still saw no one.

She opened the back door and peered out. No sooner had her nose passed the door frame, than a sudden frenzy of barking jolted her into a near heart attack. The mottled gray dog with the ragged ear lunged at her face, and she slammed the door closed, panting and leaning against the door while the dog bashed into it and barked as though possessed. As soon as she could breathe again, she teetered into a stand and tiptoed back into the kitchen.

Chopping carrots, Stefanie threw her a questioning glare.

Mari finished with the meat. For about an hour, she worked in the humid kitchen with Stefanie and the potbellied man. The white-haired woman strode in and began to speak, when the shuddering of horses' hooves sounded outside. The dogs erupted into another wild frenzy of barking.

The old woman gave a sharp exclamation and stalked from the kitchen. Mari heard something squeak, perhaps a shutter, followed by the sound of the woman's boots stamping to the front door and opening it. "Curses!" the old woman grumbled, with a trace of worry in her stern voice. "Not those ruffians!"

Mari crossed the kitchen in a flash, pulling Stefanie with her by the arm. The cook watched them, but went on with his work.

"Mari," Stefanie whispered. "What are you doing? We'll get in trouble--"

"Shifters," Mari said. "Quick, out the back while the dogs are in the front!" She ran down the hall and grabbed her cloth burrito just in case. She popped out the back door with Stephanie and they tore across the empty back yard. In a few seconds, a horrible snarling and barking began behind them. Mari looked to see two dogs hurtling around the corner of the house, their teeth bared, their eyes wild and determined.

"Go straight, there's a trail after a minute," Mari

174

gasped.

Stefanie wailed and ran faster, while Mari slowed to fling the contents of her peasant blouse behind her, across the dirt. The first dog ignored the meat offering, lunging onward as the second dog skidded into a ravenous halt and began gulping. The first dog approached Mari, now only ten feet away.

"Hold!" Mari commanded, trying to keep the fear from her voice. She pointed. "Get the meat, you idiot."

The first dog loped into an uncertain pause, and turned to see the other dog wolfing down the meat. With a rumbling snarl, the first dog raced over to the other dog. It nipped and growled, gobbling a nearby chunk of meat.

Mari ran. From the front of the cottage, she heard shouts and dogs barking. The white-haired woman's shrill arguing merged with Bierce's harsher voice, then a blast rent the air. A dog gave a horrible yelp-squeal and all at once, the dog noises quieted. A chill ran down Mari's back. *The Shifters had shot one of the dogs.*

She stumbled and ran on, breathing hard, following Stefanie. How far would they have to go before the dogs considered them too far away to chase? Off the property--out of sight? She hurled the blouse into a bush. At last, she reached the trail with Stefanie.

"Keep going!" Mari said. "It sounded like the Shifters shot one of the dogs."

"Good," Stefanie said savagely, panting. "I hope it was the one with the ragged ear. I hate that dog."

Mari didn't answer. They used their remaining breath to speed along the trail. Fortunately, no dogs were chasing them. But the Shifters were on horseback, and she didn't know if they would search the yard and trails. It all depended on what the white-haired woman told them, since she seemed adamant about holding onto new slaves. At the very least, Sanjen would get his horse back, since it was tied up in plain sight on one side of the farmhouse. Bierce would surely confiscate it.

After a few minutes, Mari looked at the trail behind her. She squinted, her heart speeding into an instant, fearful pounding. Had that been a flash of black she'd glimpsed through the trees?

"Stephanie," she whispered as she jogged. "Climb a tree. I think Shifters are coming."

"You've got to be kidding, Stratton," Stephanie said, but dashed to a leafy tree and pulled herself into it. Mari swung into another tree and tried to quiet her breathing. If the Shifters had glimpsed her or Stefanie on the trail, the hunt would be over shortly.

After a minute, two Shifters on horseback trotted single-file along the trail. From Mari's perch in the tree, it looked like the riders were Zander and the woman Morris.

"We've gone far enough," Morris was saying. "I don't know what you saw, but I don't see the farm girl. She probably went the other direction."

"Then Bierce and Markus will find her."

"Who says she took the trail, anyway? She could be hiding in the cornfield for all we know, and escaping while we search here."

Zander scratched his goatee. "Yeah. And I'd like to get back to the Fortress and see what's up with Sanjen. It doesn't make sense that his horse would end up here."

"Simple. That Tony kid rode the horse to the farm and helped the girl escape."

"Right." Zander gave a short laugh. "Like he'd be able to get out of the dungeon cell."

Shrugging, Morris guided her horse into a turn. "There's one way to find out if I'm right."

With a loud grunt, Zander turned his horse around too. They rode off the way they'd come, toward the farm.

A scant twenty seconds later, Stefanie's tree rustled and shook. She swung down and motioned to Mari with an impatient wave. "Let's get going," she whisper-hissed.

Mari climbed down. "For Pete's sake, you could've given them more time to ride enough away," she grumbled. "They could look back, you know."

Stefanie shot her a withering glare. "Whatever. So where does this stupid trail lead?" she asked as they started jogging again. "Do you have a plan?"

"Yes. This trail leads to the road north of Permandy, which leads to the cave. Randall and Lauren are there, and hopefully Tony will be there too."

"Why the cave?" Stefanie asked, distaste saturating her voice.

"The big triangle in the cave is the Portal to this dimension. We have to activate it and get back home before the Shifters find us."

"Portal," Stefanie scoffed. "Like, I'm sure."

"Believe what you want, then," Mari said shortly. Man. A little adversity sure hadn't worn any rough edges off Stefanie's personality.

They jogged on, stopping a couple of times to rest. After a while the woods thinned, and the trail began a gradual climb. Through the gaps in the trees and bushes, Mari saw the rooftops of cottages and a bustling marketplace. Her nose wrinkled at the faint but distinct smell of greasy charcoal in the air. Yep, they were passing Permandy. Soon they'd be at the golden road, and on the last leg of the journey before reaching home.

Home. She hardly dared to think of the word, after nearly a week in this dimension.

In about fifteen minutes, the trail angled and fizzled out, like an arm pointing to freedom that had disintegrated. Across a short expanse of emerald green grass, the golden road lay, with the right fork avoiding and circling the Fraghdom Forest. The left fork merged into the evil shortcut through the Fraghdom Forest, swallowed by gloomy blackness after a few feet. Mari saw Stefanie glance at the tangle of dark trees and shudder as they ran across the grass.

They reached the road and took the right fork.

Stefanie glanced back down the hill at Permandy and the valley below, resumed running, and did a double-take. "Mari," she said, slowing to a halt, a tremor in her voice. "What's that black cluster beyond Permandy? See, on the road with the cloud of dust."

Mari spun. "I don't see anything. Wagons, sheep, townspeople looking like ants--" Her words choked off as she saw what Stefanie had described. There, south of Permandy near the Haven, a shifting mass of black rode, kicking up a turbulent dust.

Shifters.

"No!" Mari cried. "Not already. They've been to the Fortress, and they know we're all free and heading to the cave." Though it was impossible to tell at this distance, Sanjen probably rode with them, too.

"Great going, Mari." Stefanie growled. "I want to go home, not be stuck in some freaking Shifter dungeon like Tony was."

Mari glared. Like it was her fault? Who needed her father around to make her feel lousy, when she had Stefanie? She threw a panicked glance at the road ahead of them, then at the Shifters. In probably less than fifteen minutes, the Shifters would reach them. "No," she said, "if all five of us are at the cave, they won't put us in a dungeon. They'll travel through the Portal with

178

us, which will wipe out part of our minds."

"Oh! So what'll we do?" Stefanie said, her face pale. "Hide in the trees again?"

Mari's thoughts whirled, trying to think of a solution. Hiding in the trees wouldn't help much, because the Shifters would ride on to capture Randall, Lauren, and Tony at the cave. It would be near-impossible for her and Stefanie to help the others escape. Her eyes snagged on the fork in the golden road, thirty feet behind them. She swallowed. Hard. She took a huge breath, a breath that felt monumentally crucial--like sucking in air before diving into a deep, deep body of water to reach something at the bottom.

"No," Mari said. "We're going to run like crazy, and take the shortcut through the Fraghdom Forest."

Chapter 17

"We're going to *what?*" Stefanie repeated, aghast. "You're certifiable!"

Mari grabbed Stefanie's arm and hauled her toward the fork that disappeared into the Fraghdom Forest. "It's our only chance. Believe me, I'm not thrilled with the idea, either."

Stefanie uttered a mangled noise and spouted off an unrepeatable stream of words as they plunged into the clammy coldness of the forest. The gloom wrapped like dead fingers around Mari's body, smothering her nose and mouth with the putrid smell of decay. Shadowy clumps rustled, legged things skittered.

Mari bent to snatch two broken branches from the ground, and gave one to Stefanie. "Here, use this to hit the spiders. They die like vampires, and they hate wood."

Stefanie clutched her branch and threw fearful glances into the murky undergrowth. "If they hate wood, why are they living in the forest with all these trees?"

"Got me. I guess they live in the bushes and avoid the trees." Mari squinted. The forest crowded in on them, growing denser as they ran, squeezing the light from the air. The glittery road narrowed into a dull, three-foot path littered with leaves and pine needles. The bushes wiggled as though alive. The ground appeared to writhe.

"What's on the ground between the bushes?" Stefanie asked, her voice wavering.

"Dunno," Mari said. "I'm trying not to look."

A black shape scuttled across the path in front of them, followed by another. Mari whacked at one with her branch, and it shrank away, rolling and convulsing.

More darted out from behind snarls of bushes, hobbling on wicked legs toward them.

"Spiders!" Stefanie shrieked, swiveling and bumping into Mari.

"Hit them with your branch," Mari said, "and don't stop moving!"

Stefanie swung her branch. They stumbled onward, dodging the spiders they could, and kicking or whacking the rest. Stefanie's voice grew hoarse from screaming. Mari clenched her teeth to stay silent. She couldn't freak out, because if she did, Stefanie might totally lose it.

A distant noise began. Eerie, undulating, like a high-pitched coyote howl, or a mentally disturbed hyena. Goosebumps rippled over Mari's entire body, even her scalp and feet. Oh no. Howling shadows. Blast Randall and his twisted science fiction novel he'd left lying around for her to read.

She saw a clump of purplish mushrooms at the base of a tree, and grimaced. She supposed those were acid mushrooms, which squirted corrosive juices upon the slightest contact. Hopefully, she and Stefanie wouldn't accidentally touch one of them.

The number of spiders increased. The hideous creatures bounced off her shoes as she ran, and one became tangled in her laces. Another latched onto her jeans and started to climb her leg. She screamed and hit it with her branch. As she knocked another spider from the path, she got a good look at the swarming ground by the bushes. Legs. Millions and trillions of legs, with shiny bodies, slithering over the ground and edging onto the path.

Zillipedes. Now she remembered them, and why they'd sounded familiar. They were like a centipede or a millipede, only longer and with more legs. With

181

leechlike suckers underneath. She'd read about them in a creepy story she'd found online two years ago, posted on some loony girl's blogsite. The story had given her a nightmare, with a dream of zillipedes crawling all over her body and into her mouth, nose, and ears.

"Oh, *sick*," she said, her chest feeling tight. How much farther did they have to go in this forest? Her adrenalin wasn't going to last much longer.

They tried to run faster, but the hordes of spiders hampered her. Stefanie swiped at two spiders, missed, and reeled off the path to avoid them. She slipped on the shifting carpet of zillipedes and fell with a squishing thump, her branch bouncing from her hand and landing a few feet away. Wasting no time, the two vampire spiders scurried over, leaping onto her legs and climbing up to her shirt.

"They're on me!" Stefanie screeched. "Get them off, get them off!"

Mari dashed over and knocked one off with her branch. The other spider zipped up to Stefanie's neck, where it huddled, twitching its black legs and starting to bite. Stefanie's screams went beyond hysterical. Mari whapped it with her branch. The spiders' legs curled, detaching as if she'd touched it with poison. She yanked Stefanie into a stand, brushing zillipedes off Stefanie's clothing with her branch, swiping frantically. Stefanie, not knowing they were leechlike, knocked them off with her bare hands. Luckily, none attached to her hands.

"Stay on the path," Mari advised, trembling as much as Stefanie.

Breaking into gulping sobs, Stefanie retrieved her branch and shook the zillipedes off. "I am *so* going to need more therapy after this. That spider *nibbled* on me, and my neck hurts. This was a monumentally bad, bad idea. If we ever get out of this freaking forest alive, I'm never speaking to you again."

"No loss," Mari retorted. "You didn't talk to me much in the first place." She hadn't known Stefanie was already in therapy, but she didn't have time to contemplate the thought further, because right then a cluster of vampire spiders skittered toward her. She focused on the accuracy of her hits. One by one, she knocked the repulsive beasts off the path.

She bashed spiders with Stefanie for quite some time, while the high-pitched howls increased in volume. Another chill washed over Mari. She glanced back. Thick, oily columns drifted after them, following them.

Stefanie stared at a nearby howling shadow and stopped cold in the path, dropping to her knees and covering her head with her arms. "Noooo, I can't take it anymore," she moaned, sobbing. "The shadow things and the spiders--all those gross bugs with way too many creepy legs--"

"Get up!" Mari cried, grabbing Stefanie's upper arm and trying to pull her to a stand. "We have to get out of here."

The thick shadow coiled closer to the path. The chill of maniacal laughter went right through Mari's body, and she saw the shadow grow knobby, gruesome hands, then long fingers. The fingers stretched toward her and Stefanie.

Stefanie stayed on her knees, whimpering and rocking, her head bent.

"*Stefanie*," Mari shouted. "We need to keep running!" She tugged on Stefanie's arm, hard, losing her balance and falling to one knee. Her hand slammed onto the ground by the path, and found a mushy hole.

An occupied hole.

With a smothered scream, Mari snatched her hand

183

out, finding it covered with thumbnail-sized vampire spiders. Teeming and hairy, the babies bit her hand like a horde of nightmare mosquitoes. She lunged to her feet and scraped at her hand with panicked swipes of her stick, knocking them off.

The shadow that had grown hands howled like a deranged coyote, drifting a mere foot away from Stefanie. Mari whacked one last baby spider from her hand and flicked a few zillipedes from her jeans. She hit spiders off Stefanie's jeans, and dug her fingers into Stefanie's bicep.

"Get up!" she yelled, shaking Stefanie as vigorously as she could. "Or I swear, Stefanie Anders, I will slap your face."

The shaking, however, seemed to be enough. With a jolt, Stefanie broke off her hysterical sobs and looked up with red-rimmed eyes. Robot-like, she unfolded to a stand and stumbled away from the shadow, jabbing stiffly at spiders with her branch.

"Good job," Mari exclaimed, her eyes streaming tears of relief. "You can do it, Stefanie. Hang in there just a little longer. Please." She knocked one spider into a nearby tree, flinching as it hit an acid mushroom and became drenched by a hissing stream of gray. The spider wilted and lay still.

Apparently, wood wasn't the only thing that could kill a vampire spider.

Mari ran with Stefanie, her nerves shot, her adrenalin long gone. She'd bitten her tongue at least three times. After what seemed like a horrendous eternity, the path widened and the gloom lightened. The howling of the shadows faded and grew silent. The path became easier to navigate as the number of spiders decreased.

"We made it," Mari said after a bit. "Look, Stefanie,

we made it."

Stefanie didn't answer, but her face relaxed and her shoulders drooped. She flung her branch away as they burst out of the Fraghdom Forest and into the warmth of welcome sunlight.

Throwing a nervous look down the golden road to check for Shifters, Mari saw none. She ditched her branch. They jogged numbly past the charred skeleton of Pod's burned cottage, and crossed the hilly fields by the rockface that led up to the cave.

"There it is," Mari said. "Home stretch. We should make it now."

Stefanie threw her a wooden look as they ran. The sound of grass whipping against their shoes and shins matched the in-and-out hissing of their breath. Mari's palms slapped onto the hard surface of the boulders when she reached the base of the mountainside, and she looked up. The slope rose high above them. Ugh. She hoped she had enough strength left to climb.

They picked their way upward, Mari's arms and legs shaking and exhausted. Loose stones bounced behind her.

A little over halfway up, she squinted at the cave opening. "Randall, Lauren," she shouted. "Tony!" A sudden wave of dread hit her. *Tony.* What if Tony hadn't made it back to the cave? All their efforts would be for nothing--their narrow escape from the farm, risking the terrors of the Fraghdom Forest, even Tony's escape from the Fortress. They wouldn't be able to activate the Portal and go home. They'd be captured when the Shifters arrived.

"Please be here, Tony. Please be here," she chanted as she scrabbled over the rocks.

"Randall!" Stefanie said.

Mari looked up to see Randall standing at the cave

185

entrance. At the same time, the distant shudders of galloping horses reached her ears.

"Hurry," Randall called down, his voice tense. "I see Shifters coming."

"Where's Tony?" Mari yelled, glimpsing Lauren's straw-blonde hair. "Is he there?"

"Yes," Randall called. At the same time, Tony's dark figure appeared next to Randall.

Tony scurried down the mountainside, giving Mari a wide grin. "You made it. I told Randall you would." He moved past her to help Stefanie, who had slowed and fallen behind. "I'll help Stefanie first."

"Okay," Mari said, "but it's not over yet." She threw a glance over her shoulder. The Shifters rode in a frenzied gallop toward them, pounding over the golden road to reach the grassy hills. The spider bite on her wrist throbbed, as did the pinprick bites from the baby spiders on her other hand. Fatigue dragged her body into a lethargic crawl. She felt as though she moved in slow motion, like in a bad dream where her limbs moved much too slowly for some approaching doom.

Tony and Stefanie caught up with her and passed her. She heard new scrabbling noises on the stones above her. Dazed, she lifted her head to see Randall's arm reaching out for her, his hand closing in a firm grasp around her arm. "Come on, Mari, you can make it."

Glad for his strength and help, she let him pull her up. He helped her climb to the top. She stumbled across the flat area in front of the cave, and swung back to check on the Shifters. They'd already crossed the hills and were dismounting, about to climb the mountainside.

"We have to activate the Portal, quick," Mari said. "It's the triangle mark on the wall."

"Let's go," Randall said, leading them into the darkness of the cave, feeling his way along the inner walls.

They progressed through the cave like a line of five blind people, hands on each other's shoulders. Behind Randall, Mari drew in a shaky breath. No flashlights this time. Good thing the Portal mark was gouged into the wall, so they could find it.

They reached the Portal. The lines of the triangle began to glow as she and Randall touched the markings, green and eerie in the blackness of the cave. Lauren, Tony, and Stefanie crowded around.

"Everyone, touch an inner triangle," Mari said hurriedly. "One each. That will activate the Portal and get us back to our own dimension."

Someone shuffled next to her. Another triangle glowed to life above Mari's, and in the pale light, Stefanie's face was visible. Other triangles became visible, and Tony reached up to the top and placed his hand on the final triangle. A faint wind began. Behind them, through the tunnel of the cave, Mari heard the Shifters shouting as they climbed the craggy rockface. They sounded close. She willed the Portal to draw them in fast, and braced herself for the hurricane of wind, motion, and sound that would come.

It didn't come. Nothing more happened besides the bright greenish glow and the rush of light wind.

"What's the matter?" Stefanie shrieked. "Is it broken?"

"I--I don't know," Mari said. "Sanjen said to touch the triangles and it would transport us." She racked her memory. Had Sanjen said or implied that anything else was needed for activation? He'd also said he'd never seen it done, so perhaps it was possible he didn't have all the information.

187

"Do we need to have everything we came with?" Randall asked. "If we do, we're in trouble, because I don't have my money, and we don't have the two flashlights or my coat."

"Or my new coat," Stefanie growled, and muttered a swear word.

"Maybe it's the opposite," Lauren said. "Maybe we can't take anything *from* this dimension. Like that cloak Kale gave you, Randall."

Randall flung off his cloak. "Anyone else?"

"My monk robe is already off," Lauren said.

"I have plenty of dirt from this dimension on me," Stefanie said dryly.

Randall returned his hand to his triangle section. Again, nothing more happened.

The Shifter's shouts became louder, echoing into the mouth of the cave.

"They're here," Tony said. "Think, Mari. What else did Sanjen tell you about the Portal?"

"Nothing," Mari cried, her nerves disintegrating with the sounds of boot scrapings and Shifter voices. "He said it glowed when we touched it, and if Shifters came with us, the dreaming parts of our minds would be erased. He told me how this dimension is formed from our dreams and nightmares. This dimension has lots of landscapes like this one, which are made up of the Builder's dreams and nightmares--" She broke off with a sharp cry, an image of the sketches on the shed workbench flashing into her mind.

In those sketches, the top triangle had been outlined darker than the rest of the triangles.

And she was the Builder.

She grabbed Tony's hand from the top triangle and switched it to her section. She slammed her own hand onto the top section, and immediately the wind increased to a blasting rush, then to a dizzying howl.

The green glow flared. Mari felt her arm being pulled, hard, as if the triangle were sucking it inward by magnetic pull. The sounds of the Shifters in the cave tunnel faded. Mari pressed closer together with the others, melted into the Portal, blasted through unknown spaces. Someone screamed. Intense pressure churned with the roaring wind.

And then all was deafeningly still, as though nothing had ever happened.

Chapter 18

Mari shook her head, opening her eyes and raking her hair from her face with trembling fingers. She stood with the others in an odd sort of group hug, upright in the semi-darkness of somewhere. Stefanie's hair was fanned across Tony's shoulder, and one of Lauren's arms was wrapped around Mari's waist.

The others grunted and groaned and shifted.

"We made it!" Lauren breathed. "We're back in the shed."

"What?" Mari said, looking around. Sure enough, the dim shapes of dusty shelves surrounded them, and rays of two flashlights beamed across the floor. Randall walked over and kicked a third flashlight out from under the workbench.

"Wow," Randall said. "Talk about turbo long-life batteries. I gotta get me some of these."

Tony picked up another flashlight and shined it onto Stefanie. "How's your neck?" he asked. "I noticed it was bleeding a little, before, like it got scraped."

"Yeah, from those danged spiders in the forest," Stefanie said, then gasped as her hands felt her neck. "I can't believe it--it doesn't hurt, and I can't feel the scraped-up place where they nibbled on me."

"There's nothing on your neck now," Tony said.

Mari grabbed the third and final flashlight and checked her own wrist. All clear. No wound, no blood. No tiny pricks all over her other hand, either. "When we came back through the Portal, we left our injuries behind," she said in amazement.

"Fine with me," Randall said with a grunt. "My back was killing me where that foreman took a swipe at me with his whip. Our shirts are still shredded though, Tony."

190

"Bummer," Tony said. "Mamá is going to kill me. I'm not sure how I'm going to explain that. She'll never let me come to a party again."

Lauren pushed up her sweater sleeve. "But I still have the Portal mark on my arm." She sounded tired.

"Me too." Tony put a hand on Stefanie's shoulder. "So, you girls really went through the Fraghdom Forest?" he asked, throwing incredulous looks at her and Mari.

Mari nodded. "It's the only reason we made it in time."

"Yeah, Mari's lame idea," Stefanie said with a sniff. "Some shortcut. Plus, I nearly got my leg chewed off escaping that farm. I swear, I'm *so* going to have post-traumatic stress after this."

"Let's get back to your house and call our parents," Lauren said. "They must be really worried."

No one argued that idea. They left the shed and trailed across the long grass and around bushes, their flashlights bobbing. The sprawling Anders house remained as lit up as when they'd departed on the night of the party. Distant cheering reached their ears.

"What's going on in your house, Stef?" Randall asked.

"No clue, Stratton," Stefanie retorted. "I just want to go inside and clean up. I haven't had a bath in almost a week, and my fingernails are broken down to ugly little stubs."

"Hey, guys," Tony said. "My watch is working now."

Mari dug her watch from her jeans pocket and checked it in the swath of her flashlight. The second hand had stopped its spastic twitch, sweeping smoothly instead, and now read a few minutes past midnight. "Mine too. I guess our watches didn't like the other

191

dimension."

"I can relate to that," Stefanie said.

Sucking in a deep breath of cool, January night air, Mari felt herself relax a little more. Her waking nightmare had ended. Life could return to its normal, Mainworld state. But the Portal mark remained seared onto her arm, the way the horror of the last week would be seared onto her mind and memories. She did wonder about Sanjen. What had he thought, when he and the other Shifters arrived a mere handful of seconds too late to accompany them through the Portal?

With the others, Mari crossed the back deck of the Anders' house. Thumping music boomed out with blasts of party horns and tweeting noisemakers as Stefanie pushed open the sliding glass door.

"There you are, Stef," one of her preppy friends said, bouncing and waving a sparkly streamer. "I wondered where you went--you missed the countdown. Happy New Year!"

Stefanie's mouth dropped open. Randall stared, and Mari stood close enough to Tony to hear him give a gulping swallow. Lauren clutched Mari's arm.

"It's still New Year's Eve?" Lauren asked in a low, disbelieving voice that was almost lost in the noise of the merriment.

"No way!" Stefanie cried. "How can that be? We've been gone almost a week."

"Major weirdness," Tony muttered. "So much for calling our parents. They didn't even know we were gone."

Mari blinked. "Wow. I guess time must flow differently in that other dimension."

"Yeah," Randall said. "Time stopped here with our watches, but it moved forward in Permandy."

They stood by the door, with the music crashing

around them like a surreal theme song. Mari's gaze slid to a view of part of the dancefloor. There, Brad and Susan were engaged in a sensual lip-lock that rivaled a soap opera embrace. Mari shrugged, her heart and emotions past caring. Brad? Such a shallow guy. His treachery seemed eons ago. A fresher treachery and heartache had replaced his.

Stefanie gave a grating growl. "So how did all this insanity happen tonight? Since Mr. Simpson hid the ping-pong balls for us, and drew those triangles in his shed, does he know about the Portal?"

"Good question," Randall said, and Tony nodded.

"Let's go ask him," Lauren said, her voice firm. "Right now. Think he stayed up until midnight?"

Stefanie looked at Lauren as if for the first time. "Yes, that's a great idea. Follow me, you guys. We're going to pay a visit to Mr. Simpson."

"Aw, come on," Mari said, her heartbeat increasing in tempo again. "Can't it wait 'til tomorrow or the next day?"

No one answered her. She sighed and followed them as they went back out the sliding glass door and down the car-packed driveway. Shivering and wrapping her arms around herself, she watched the shadowy fieldgrass as it rippled and writhed in the brisk wind. She eyed her mother's car with longing as they passed it parked on the street. With Stefanie leading, they made their way up a long gravel driveway to an older two-story house with a wide front porch.

The lights of the house glowed like an unwanted beacon, beckoning them forward like sleepwalkers. Yes, Mr. Simpson had stayed awake. Against her will, Mari trudged up the porch steps and stood close to Lauren for warmth while Stefanie punched the doorbell with a determined finger. Silence met the faint echoing ring for a number of seconds, then the clomping of approaching footsteps sounded inside. Mari's gaze wandered around the clean porch and the door, and all at once she froze, petrified in one chilling instant.

Across the top of the door, a large gold triangle decorated the doorframe.

"You guys," she hissed. "There's a triangle above the door."

No one had time to respond. The door opened, well-oiled and soundless. A gaunt, shrewd-looking man moved into the doorway, partially revealed by the porch light yet partially silhouetted by the backlight of his dwelling. He wore half-glasses, and his ears lay so flat to his head they looked like a hissing cat's. "Can I help you?" he asked, and added, "Ah, good evening, Miss Anders." His gaze raked over Stefanie.

"We want to know what those drawings in your shed mean," Stefanie said, without greeting or any other preamble. "The ones of the triangles."

Mr. Simpson's thin eyebrows arched in amusement, and his mouth quirked. "Why, those drawings, my dear, are merely a hobby of mine. Why do you ask?"

Stefanie put one hand on her hip. "Look at me. My hair is gross, my jeans are dirty. Do I look like I've been to a party? No, because I've been gone almost an entire week instead. To some blasted place where vampire spiders bite your neck, and people lock you up and make you work like a slave. I bet you know about the Portal and how we got to that other dimension, and we want more information."

Mari exchanged a sideways glance with Lauren. Maybe someone else should have done the talking. If Mr. Simpson had no idea about the Portal, that spiel would sound pretty loony.

Breaking out into a dry chuckle, Mr. Simpson

194

folded his arms across his chest. "You think my drawings have something to do with what you describe? It sounds, Miss Anders, as though you've fallen asleep somewhere and had a bad dream. Or perhaps you've been sampling some of your father's gin and tonic, yes?"

"Take a hike," Stefanie snarled. "I'll tell you what you can do with your--"

"Thanks, Mr. Simpson," Tony interrupted. "We were just wondering about the triangles, because after being in your shed, we ended up with these." He rolled up his sleeve and showed the gaunt man the mark branded onto his forearm.

Mr. Simpson leaned forward and peered over his half-glasses. His eyes seemed to glitter in the porch light. "A triangle of five, eh?" he muttered. He straightened, with the quirk of a grin still lingering upon his face. "A curious mark, for certain. Amazing, what tattoos you young people get these days."

"We didn't put these on our arms, and they're not tattoos," Randall said. "It's a mark that looks like the Portal. Did your drawings cause the Portal to be activated somehow?"

"Randall," Mari cut in. "We should drop this. Because obviously, we're not getting anywhere." She didn't like the man's smug, secretive manner and didn't think he was telling the truth, but she'd had enough. What did it matter now, anyway?

"True," Mr. Simpson agreed, his eyes narrowing a little as he looked at Mari. "This conversation is pointless. You kids are here twenty minutes after midnight, interrogating a lone, middle-aged man with silly questions. You're young. Go enjoy your party, and celebrate your youth while you can."

Next to Mari, Lauren gave a deep sigh. "Sorry to

have bothered you, Mr. Simpson. Good night, and Happy New Year."

Mr. Simpson's hint of a smile twitched and spread across his face, wide.

"Happy New Year, to all five of you," he said, and closed the door.

The End

Junction 2020: The Portal is the first book of a five-part series, with each book written from the viewpoint of one of the five main characters. The next book in the series involves Tony's harrowing experiences, and is called *Junction 2020: Nightmare Realization.*

Carol Riggs

Visit my website at www.carolriggs.com

5965946R0

Made in the USA
Charleston, SC
27 August 2010